END OF THE TUNNEL

THE MADELINE JOURNEYS BOOK 4

P. A. WILSON

FREE EBOOK

Claim your copy of Obstacles of Magic when you use the QR code to sign up for my newsletter and learn more about Madeline's history with magic.

1

It had been two months since her party had arrived in the elven homeland. A beautiful area of rolling hills and small lakes surrounded by giant willows, and something that looked like a magnolia, but had tiny flowers. The library was set in a small grove. Domed roofs of the clustered buildings dwarfed by the ancient trees. The rooms were filled with scrolls and books preserved by a spell that kept the air dry.

Madeline remembered feeling both awe and crashing disappointment when she first stepped foot in this room. Awe for the sheer age of the knowledge contained in the room, and disappointment because she wouldn't be able to read any of them. She'd learn to speak the common language, but reading was a whole other skill. Each race had its own script, and none of them made sense to her. Amberbirch had solved the problem. Taking a thin sheet of paper, and speaking a few words over it, she handed it to Madeline. "This will help you understand what is written. Place it on top of the page you wish to read, and it will become clear to you."

Since then, Madeline had been able to read the words, but

most had not become clear. They were running out of time to close the gate between worlds before the next battle started.

"Another dead end, Madeline?" Amberbirch asked as she entered the room. The elven woman was small. Elves are about two thirds of the size and mass of a human. They appeared ageless at first to Madeline. Dressed in a loose gown that was the same color as the deepest part of the lake, with her hair braided in a complicated pattern that reached her hips, Amberbirch gave the impression of being willowy, but without the height.

"Not exactly," she answered, rubbing her back to ease the stiffness from bending over the scroll for so long. "I think I may have found more details of the past invasions, but some of the writing is faded so much that I can barely read it."

Behind Amberbirch came a servant bearing food, caf, and wine. Jode joined them as the servant finished laying out the meal.

"I can have someone rewrite it," Amberbirch offered. "Elven eyes are sharper. It may help."

"I don't think we have time for a rewrite." Madeline looked at the piles of books in the room, knowing she didn't have time to read all of them once. The gate would open soon, and if she didn't find a way to seal it, everyone here would die in the battle. They would only be the first of thousands. "I'll take it outside tomorrow. The sun will help make the words more clear."

Amberbirch reached for Madeline's hand to help her rise, but she waved it away, reluctant to rely on others until she really was unwieldy with pregnancy. The small bump was getting to the point where she'd soon have to find a different posture. She had already had to give up riding, she was going to cling to the last shreds of independence as long as she could.

Jode touched her shoulder to pull her attention away from the pile of books. "You are tired. When did you last eat?"

Madeline pushed back from the table, loath to abandon her studies, but knowing she was getting tired and needed a break. "I guess I could do with a real meal. Perhaps I can come back to this later."

Jode took her arm and led her to the table, his assistance always welcome. "We will eat together. Tell me what you found, and we may be able to discover a truth between us that is hidden to you."

"Don't you get tired of talking about this?" Madeline longed for a time when she could sit alone with her husband and talk about anything, or nothing.

"It is not a subject we can avoid, so let us embrace it. If I am unable to help, it will be of value to have Amberbirch hear what you think you have learned. Perhaps you understand a different meaning because you come from a different world."

Madeline knew that it was certain that she had a different understanding. "It's probably why I get to be The Chosen One. My misunderstanding will uncover the secret."

Amberbirch poured caf for Madeline and wine for herself and Jode. "You are both right," she said. "Without discussion, you will never know if there is a difference between what you understand and what we do."

Taking a sandwich from Jode, Madeline gathered her thoughts and quelled an odd feeling that she should keep her information close. This was the same as when she did a case review with her colleagues at home – no, on earth – no, the other earth. Oh shit. "Let's start from the beginning," she said. "You know that there are supposed to be multiple universes."

Jode nodded and added, "When worlds come close enough, a gate opens allowing people to cross. But only warlike people seem to come here. It is odd that only the elves seem to know this."

Madeline looked at Amberbirch who was studying her glass of wine. If the elven woman had nothing to offer, then there was probably no difference yet to be discussed. "Yes, this is the first time that people outside the elven world have been brought in to help."

Amberbirch looked at them. "It has been the duty of the elves to save the world since time began. I will be happy to have you succeed, Madeline, but the army will come in case we have to do our duty."

"Some of the invaders survive," Madeline said ignoring the implied dig at her ability.

Smiling at them, Amberbirch straightened a fold in her robe. "The Tryll haven't yet integrated."

Not understanding why the woman was suddenly undermining them, Madeline responded, "If the elves kept this a secret, how did the others explain new types of people showing up?"

Amberbirch rose and bowed to Madeline. "I think we are both feeling the stress of our study. Perhaps, it would be better if Jode acted as your sounding board." Without waiting for either of them to respond, she gracefully exited the room.

Shocked at the change in Amberbirch, Madeline looked at Jode to see him frowning. The woman had never been anything but a gracious host. Although the library wasn't her home, she was there to mentor and guide Madeline as she searched for ways to fulfill the prophecy. "What just happened? Did I step over some line of etiquette?"

Jode still stared at the archway, apparently as surprised as Madeline at the reaction. He shook his head as if trying to bring himself back to the present. "Not one that I am aware of," he said. "Perhaps she took your words to mean that the elves should have asked for help. It is clear they are proud of their role as safe keepers."

"So much for getting help." Madeline placed her empty mug on the tray for the servants to clear later. "I have only found hints and clues that there is an answer. I think that we need to return to the gate."

"I do not like that place." Jode stood and walked to the

window. "I always feel that we are under attack when we are there."

They had been there only twice, but she knew the feeling he meant. A feeling of being watched, of evil waiting for a moment of indecision, or inattention. "We will have to go there, Jode." She joined him at the window and patted his hand, a gesture meant to reassure, but it didn't help quell the dread that had crept over her with his words. "I don't think we can hope that the answer is here. That we will just have to go to the circle with the solution."

"It is not just your life I worry about."

She turned to look at the table of books. "I know. It's everyone's life."

"I meant the children."

Feeling guilty that they hadn't been her first thought, Madeline turned back to Jode. "Yes, but if I don't fix this, they will die." The words hurt to say. The thought of her babies in danger chilled her body from the inside.

"It is not something I can think about," Jode said, joining her back at the books. "Shall I stay?"

She warmed at the thought of company. "If you find sitting watching me read interesting, I would love you to stay. It gets lonely in here."

He pulled a chair from the corner and sat beside her. "You can tell me what you are reading. We will discuss the meanings as you find them."

Madeline pulled the next book on the pile toward her, opening it to the first page. Placing her translation sheet on the title page she read aloud. *"The life of Timberraven, a scholar of the last invasion."*

Turning to next page, she slipped the translation sheet on top. The words blurred, something that happened in about half the books she read. Then the words came into focus in patches. It took a few minutes to get all of the words clear enough to read, the final ones flickering a few times before settling.

"I don't know if that means anything," she said when Jode asked if it was normal. "I'll ask Amberbirch, but not just now. I think she needs a bit of alone time."

"Let someone else smooth the way for you."

Madeline let the tension she was feeling out in a laugh. "I can be tactful," she said when she had her laughter under control.

"Yes, you can, but you don't have to do everything. Regis and Springheart can do more than just help you read documents."

Madeline agreed, not really believing she could delegate any of the important tasks. Whatever had twisted Amberbirch's panties was probably something simple. Having to help The Chosen One find a way to seal the gate, was probably almost as stressful as being The Chosen One. "Why don't you get them doing that? I'd rather she was back to her pleasant self tomorrow at the gate. Like you say, it feels like there's already an enemy waiting to attack there. We don't need to bring any animosity with us."

Jode kissed her and left with a promise to return and help. As soon as she was alone, Madeline put aside the book she'd been reading and started flipping through her notes. They were going to the circle of stones that formed the entrance to the gate between worlds. She didn't have any information on how to seal the gate, but there was a book that described the gate, and the construction. There had to be something useful in there, something to guide them tomorrow.

She found the notes and the book and had them laid out and was settling in when Amberbirch joined her. "I apologize for my behavior," she said from the archway. It felt as though she was waiting for permission to enter the room.

Madeline stepped away from the papers she'd spread out, knowing that if she sat at the table, her attention would wander to the information. She'd already done something to upset Amberbirch. She wasn't willing to chance doing it again.

"We are all tired and tense," Madeline said as she approached.

"Let's just forget about what happened." She took the woman's hand and drew her into the room. Telling Amberbirch about the planned trip in the morning, Madeline asked about the problem with the translation page.

Amberbirch frowned. "It should not happen. Please, show me."

Digging out *The Life of Timberraven*, Madeline repeated the exercise. The page became clear immediately. Annoyed, Madeline turned the page and said, "Let me try a fresh page."

The next page came clear immediately, as did the following five pages. "Great, it's not going to happen while you're here."

Amberbirch took the translation sheet from Madeline. Holding it up to the light coming through the window, she placed her hand on the page and muttered some words. "I have recharged the spell, but this fuzziness should not be happening at all. Let me know as soon as it does in the future."

Madeline nodded and hoped that it would happen soon.

2

*T*he evening came too soon for Madeline. No matter how many candles were lit, there was never enough light to bring out the faded words on the pages in front of her. She'd triggered many a headache trying to puzzle out the meanings of the texts.

She stretched and heard her bones crack from being held in one position too long. Regis and Springheart were huddled over other scrolls, making notes now and then. The frowns on their faces showed their lack of progress. "I think we need to find another way to do this research," she said. "We don't have time to read all these books and scrolls. And without an index or something, we'll just be feeling around in the dark."

The two looked up from their work. Springheart slight and blond, Regis not much bigger, but dark haired, they could have been brothers. At one time, she'd suspected they were, but now that she'd seen more elves, there was no doubt that Springheart was a full elf and Regis was all human.

"What do you have in mind?" Regis asked. "My magic is at your disposal if that will help."

Regis carried powerful magic. Even when she'd seen how

complicated it was to wield three types of magic, Madeline had been jealous of his talent. The babies growing inside her continued to hold her magic hostage. There was no guarantee that she would ever regain the power. It was a hole inside her. The power only flowed through her for a short time, but it had become so much a part of her that she didn't feel like herself without it.

"I wish I did have some idea," she admitted. "All I know is we aren't getting anywhere doing this. In my old world, we had a saying, repeating the same actions and expecting different results is the definition of madness."

Springheart chuckled. "Perhaps your idea of visiting the site where the gate will open again, is the best approach. Now that we have a little information, perhaps we will gain more knowledge from the writing there."

They had visited the site of prophecy shortly after arriving at the library. A circle of a hundred stones with words written on each of the massive pavers. The words drew the reader around in a circle to the center, like a simple labyrinth. The center was a deep hole, big enough for two people, but with no way to enter other than to jump to probable death.

"Jode doesn't like the idea, but I agree." She placed her hand on her belly. It was too soon for her to feel the babies moving. It felt like there was a presence there anyway. Something that acknowledged her touch. "Regis, could you try to contact Blu? I know they are on the road to us, but if Blu has some advice, it would be better to get it now."

"I'm sure Simon and Callisra are hurrying the journey, Madeline," Regis answered. "I will try, but without an idea of where they actually are, I don't hold much hope."

Simon and Callisra had taken a lot of convincing to go and get Blu to join the party. Madeline knew that the soonest they would arrive was in a week. "We won't know unless we try."

The two men rose and held out their hands to assist her in

gaining her feet. "You should not spend the entire day sitting," Springheart said. "Pregnant women need exercise."

Madeline gave a bitter laugh. "I know. I'll get all the exercise I need when we've figured out what to do." And tomorrow she'd be on horseback, probably for the last time until after the babies came. Walking around the circle of stones would be exercise enough for now.

Springheart and Madeline joined Jode and Amberbirch who were sitting around a fire pit watching as the sun dropped behind the grove of trees. When they were seated, Amberbirch instructed the servants to bring refreshments. She had taken on the role of hostess as well as being the person who advised them.

"What have you learned today?" she asked as wine and tea were poured. "Are we any closer to stopping the next invasion?"

Glad that Amberbirch's mood had improved, Madeline wanted desperately to say yes, but she admitted it had been another day of dead ends and obscure texts. "We'll go to the site at daybreak."

Amberbirch straightened and cast her glance to Springheart. "That is a long journey if you have learned nothing to help you."

It wasn't what she wanted to hear, but Madeline couldn't find any way to argue against it. While she struggled to find a way to lighten the pessimism, Jode put his arm around Madeline and drew her close. "I think a day away from the library will do our scholar some good. We can make a picnic of it for all of us. It is not that far."

"A picnic would be fun," Madeline agreed, thinking that the circle was the last place she would choose to relax and have fun. "I'll bring my notes, and maybe we can decipher some of those words."

Amberbirch was silent and Madeline watched her fingers whiten from the tightness of her grip. No one else seemed to notice the tension. Madeline wrote it off to the same fear they all had. That the knowledge they needed would stay hidden, and there would be a battle of monstrous proportions when the gate opened.

"I think you are probably right," Amberbirch finally said. "We can take a day to get fresh air and a new perspective. I am sure that will make all the difference."

Regis joined the group taking a glass of wine and lowering himself to a brightly embroidered cushion. "I regret I was not able to contact Blu. It seems we will have to wait until they arrive."

"Thanks for trying." Madeline placed her empty teacup on the floor. The wine was tempting, and she'd been assured that it wouldn't hurt the babies, but her conditioning was that pregnant women didn't drink, so she stuck to water, or tea.

Jode gave her a gentle squeeze of reassurance. "They will arrive in time. I have every confidence in Simon. And Arabela will be mustering an army to fight the battle if needed. It has been done before. It will be done again. This time the elves will have help."

"Each time the battle becomes worse, the casualties larger," Amberbirch said. There was a tone in her voice of regret, some pain Madeline couldn't name. "We need to close the gate and put an end to this cycle. We may not survive this battle. Even if we do, we will definitely not survive the next."

Wiggling out of Jode's embrace, Madeline placed her hand on Amberbirch's shoulder. "We will keep trying until the end. If that is a battle, then we will win and continue to search for a way to close the gate."

The woman looked at Madeline's hand then into her eyes. Madeline saw an echo of the pain she'd heard in the words. "Let us hope your optimism isn't misplaced."

Madeline smiled. She had faced, and overcome, so many challenges since coming here that she would never have even imagined in her old world. "Optimism, or luck, it doesn't matter. We'll be successful."

3

*T*he next morning the five of them set out for the site of the gate between worlds. Jode and Madeline led them, with Amberbirch behind, Springheart and Regis following. The servants would bring lunch later, leaving them time to search for information amid the stones and ancient trees.

"Are we certain this is the right place?" Madeline asked as they entered the clearing. "It has been so long since the last passage."

"It is the place," Amberbirch answered. "I remember it. Pain, and terror, and many deaths happened because we could not close the gate. One does not forget that easily. Perhaps not ever."

Madeline glanced at the woman. Until yesterday all the emotion she'd shown was calm, peace, and welcoming. Perhaps this pain in her voice was because she had lost someone in the battle. Perhaps that is why she knew so much about the history of the passage.

The horses were left to graze in a small clearing. Springheart assured them that their mounts would not stray and didn't need to be hobbled. Madeline headed through the trees, leading the others to their destination.

She stood at the edge of the site, re-familiarizing herself with the details. Now that she was looking at it again, it was clear that this was the place. It had been a month since she'd last looked out over the shallow bowl that seemed too small to be so dangerous. It was about the size of four city blocks of concentric circles of black paving stones. Each one was engraved with a letter or word along the outer edge.

In the very center was the well. This was where the invaders would rise from, according to Amberbirch. If they were to come in full size, it would be possible to cut them down before they became too many to fight. The well would allow two humans, or possibly four creatures the size of goblins to pass. But when the invaders came, they arrived in a cloud of mites that magically formed into individuals. There was no limit to how many could come through at the same time.

They all stood facing the first stone, on which was written the elvish word danger. Or, at least, that was one of the meanings. Madeline closed her eyes and tried to access the magic that her babies had stolen. She could feel power just out of her reach, like warmth from a fire in another room.

"Shall we walk the circuit?" Amberbirch asked.

Madeline opened her eyes and looked toward the center. "Why is it necessary to walk along the path? Can we just cross to the well?"

"I do not remember anyone doing so. We always walk the circle," the elven woman said. "We read each word as we pass, taking the time to meditate as we do."

"The words make no sense that way, so let's try it from the center out." Madeline started cutting across the circles. "Do they really walk around the circle when they are preparing to fight?"

Looking behind, Madeline saw the others follow. Jode right behind her, Amberbirch behind him, Regis and Springheart in the rear, watching the area as if expecting attack.

"It is not the most useful way to defend your position," Jode said as he cast his glance around the circle.

Amberbirch lifted her skirt to take the larger steps needed to cross the stones. "The circle is filled with warriors when the gate is going to open. They will arrive within days of the deadline. If we have closed the gate, they will leave."

Madeline continued to cross. "Is it possible that the words are to be read in a different order?" There had to be a reason for the words. Why would they go to the trouble of carving the words and painting them? She heard paper crackle behind her.

Regis was sorting through the notes they had brought from the library. "I'll walk the circle and make note of each of the words in order from the outside in. We can make copies and try to create a message of them when we return. I don't know that I think clearly when we are here."

Madeline agreed with him and then strode forward, reaching the center, and turning to watch the others array themselves nearby, but as far as they could be from the edge. As though someone might reach up and grasp their ankles to drag them down to hell. She saw Regis working on the catalog of words. "Amberbirch, why are the words here? If they were a solution to the problem, they should be understandable."

"They have been there for as long as even the oldest of our people remember. In our history, we have records of experiments undertaken. The words are not instructions on closing the gate. They are not a way to stop the invaders. They are not an incantation, at least not one that helps us to avoid a fearsome battle."

Madeline looked around her. The stones seemed too perfect to be set without purpose. It wasn't useful to know what the stones weren't. They needed to know what they were.

Springheart stepped closer to the well. "Perhaps there are words inside that complete the information."

Madeline reached for his arm to keep him from entering. "We

need rope if someone is going in there. I will not lose someone to a stupid misstep."

He allowed her to pull him away from the edge. "I'll go back to the library and get some. Jode can anchor me. I will hurry. By the time Regis has recorded the words, and you have walked the circle back, I will have the means to explore the center."

Madeline was torn. She desperately wanted all the information they could gather, but she also feared what might be lurking just below their sight. Springheart didn't wait for her response. He sprang away stopping to let Regis know what he was about.

"There's nothing here to answer any of our questions," Madeline said. "Let's hope Springheart is right." She started walking the circle in reverse. As she moved, a thought occurred to her. Pointing to the word on the paver in front of her, she asked, "Amberbirch, does this mean anything different if we read it backwards?"

The elven woman stepped beside Madeline and glanced at the word carved into the stone. "Approached from the outside, this means heart. From this side, the inside, I suppose, it means family." She looked at Madeline, amazed. "This is promising, Madeline. Let's hope it isn't another dead end."

Wishing the woman would be more optimistic, Madeline continued to walk. Regis joined them on the final stone. "I've written them in a circle as they are in life." He sketched the last word and then handed the paper to Madeline. "It occurred to me that we can then read them in different configurations by moving the papers around."

Madeline looked at the sheet of paper. Regis had not only drawn the words in the spiral as they were on the stones, he'd drawn the stones in detail. "Is this to scale?" He looked at her, puzzlement on his face.

Jode looked over her shoulder and then took the paper and held it level with the stones. "Yes, it is a real representation of the stones as they lay." He turned the page so that it was aligned with the pavers beneath them. "I see what you noticed."

Madeline smiled. "Yes, we don't know what the words mean, but look how the stones form a pattern. It's broken so I can't be sure, but it does seem to mostly radiate from the center as well as spiral into it. If we can fill in the broken pieces, there will be an answer here. I know we will find it." She started walking the reverse of the pattern checking each stone and word that Regis had drawn. He had made no mistakes.

WHEN SPRINGHEART ARRIVED BACK at the camp, the others were sitting in a huddle, pouring over the notes that Madeline had created. He placed the rope on the ground and sat to join them. "Any luck? Have you found a clue?" he asked.

Madeline explained what they had discovered. "If you can see any other symbols below the well, it might help us to decipher the code."

He gathered the rope and some of the blank pages along with a pen. "I will do as Regis has done."

Jode rose to accompany Springheart, but Regis halted him. "I'll take the rope. If Springheart has any questions, I am the best person to answer. Why don't you create copies of my drawing while we are gone? It may only be a few minutes if there is nothing below the well."

Springheart looked at Regis. He was not as muscular as Jode. "Will you be able to hold my weight if I need to be inside more than a few minutes?"

Regis laughed. "I am stronger than I look. And I thought if you need me to, I can take my turn down the well. You will be able to bear my weight much better than you could Sir Jode's."

Springheart accepted the logic. "Then let us go. We should walk around the path rather than cut across. If there is writing inside the well, it might make sense if we have seen the words that lead to it."

Regis took the rope. "Lead the way."

There was room for them to walk together along the pavers. Springheart silently read the words as they walked around the first circuit. He was happy to continue in silence, in contemplation, but Regis started talking as they entered the second orbit of the path.

"Have you explored in this type of space before?"

Springheart glanced up at Regis. "Are you worried about entering a dark and confined space?"

Regis laughed. "No, I have spent enough time in small dark corners. I would be more worried if there was any chance of something coming from the other side."

Springheart tried not to think of the possibility of entering the well too close to the time it became the gate. "Yes, but we have plenty of time before that will happen." Springheart glanced at the words carved into the stones before them. Even with the new ideas, he could discern no meaning. "And if we cannot seal the gate, we will not stand alone. Every elf family will stand to defend Cartref from invasion."

Regis stepped to the next stone. "They won't stand alone this time. Perhaps that will make a difference."

Springheart did not hold out much hope, but didn't want to voice that fear. "Perhaps."

"Why haven't the elves asked for help before?"

"I do not know. This is lore passed from parent to child. Perhaps I would have received it from my mother if she had survived."

"Sorry, I didn't mean to bring that up," Regis said. "Neither of us has a great family history. I'm the forgotten bastard of a noble family. You are an orphan."

Springheart laughed bitterly. "Not only an orphan, but one of a people who value family over everything. At least you can hope for some standing with Arabela when this is over." Regis looked at him with sympathy. Springheart hated that emotion. "Don't pity me. I think my future is here, either to fight and die in battle, or to help seal the gate. When we are done, I will return to my life as a wanderer. It isn't so bad."

"I can't speak for Arabela, but I think Madeline and Jode will take you into their household. Perhaps into their family." Regis clapped Springheart on his shoulder. "Family is something you can make. Look at me. Despite what I've done, Arabela is willing to take me as her family."

"Wait," Springheart said unwilling to continue talking about possibilities of a future he may not get. "Before we enter the well, let's see if we can see any pattern in the stones, or in the words, from here."

They were almost at the center, at the lowest part of the bowl, which flattened on the bottom. Springheart turned full circle. Regis followed his movement. They both surveyed the path.

"It feels like there should be something," Regis said. "As if we are just to the side of the right perspective."

Springheart agreed. "The best position would be over the well, but we have nothing to cover it, or to raise someone high enough to see the bowl from the center." He looked around the surrounding clearing. "Perhaps the center is not the right angle. When we are finished here, we should walk along the rises around this clearing."

From their position, Springheart noticed that there were regular humps in the grass. They would help in the battle to channel the enemy if they were higher. Perhaps they had filled in during the time since the last opening. "And we can return with some way of observing from the center."

Ten pavers later, they stood at the edge of the well. Springheart's instincts were trying to drive him away from the hole, but he ignored them. He lay on his stomach, head over the edge of the well. He looked up and blinked at the brightness of the day.

"Something is absorbing the light only a few feet down." Regis made to join him. "No, stay back. It would not do for both of us to fall into the hole."

He rose, and they stood a few feet away from the edge, tying one end of the rope around each of their waists. Regis backed up another paver and braced against the slight unevenness in the stones.

4

*S*pringheart checked the strength of the knot around his waist and then lowered his legs into the hole. He felt icy cold touch his feet, then his calves as he lowered the rest of his body into the darkness. When he was fully inside, he braced his back against one side by extending his legs as far as the opposite side. He worked his legs and back down a few inches.

Bone chilling cold radiated from beneath him and the lower he went, the dimmer the light became, as though the darkness was a solid object. The sun was almost directly overhead, allowing him to see the walls of the well. Stones similar to those of the path lined the walls, placed perpendicular, there were words carved, but not painted, along the first layer of stones. He took the paper and pen from within his jacket and quickly drew what he saw. Turning his head, he noticed that the words fully ringed the well. Words standing out even though the light seemed to bend the walls around him, making the shadows shift.

Springheart placed the paper and pen back into his jacket for safekeeping. Then carefully spider-walked his way around enough to face the remaining stones. He quickly sketched the final words as he struggled with his numb fingers, the strength sapped by the cold that seemed to creep up his body.

When the paper and pen were once again safely tucked into his jacket, Springheart gave the rope a tug. He felt the tension increase around his waist and started inching up the wall. He was only a few feet down the well, but the journey out seemed to take far too long for the distance.

As soon as he could, Springheart reached for the edge and pulled himself out. Just as his toes passed out of the well, a rush of wind and dust pulled at him, forcing him backwards. Unable to make headway, Springheart balanced on the edge, bent over, fingers scrabbling on the smooth stone for purchase that wasn't there. His heart thudded with panic. Reaching for a seam, or any crack, knowing there was none here at the edge, he tried to fight the pull of the wind.

Nothing worked. He was being dragged back into the void of the well. Back into the darkness and cold. He was going to die. He struggled against the feeling of defeat and the yearning to simply let go.

Suddenly a yank on the rope drew him a foot from the gaping hole and the wind died down. Regis continued to drag him until there was no danger of Springheart falling into the depths.

MADELINE RACED toward Springheart and felt the cold of his body radiate to meet her fingers, her fear screaming at her to run in the opposite direction. He was flat on his back, gasping on the stones, his, normally pale face blue. "Get a blanket," she shouted at Jode as she wrapped her arms around the elf to share her own warmth.

As she held him, he stopped gasping and the cold receded. "I will be fine, Madeline. Please allow me to stand." He struggled to his feet, but Madeline could tell that he was recovering quickly as he found his balance.

"Did you see what happened?" Regis asked. "The wind? The dust?"

Amberbirch joined them. She had not run to the scene like Madeline but had serenely crossed the stones. She handed Springheart a mug. "We did see it. What did you do to disturb it?"

Jode returned with the blanket that they had been using as a ground cover. Springheart handed Amberbirch the mug and accepted the blanket. Draping it across his shoulders, he worked to undo the knot around his waist. Springheart's fingers were still trembling, so Madeline took her belt knife and sliced the rope at the knot to release him.

The rope fell to the stones revealing the abraded length that had been at his back. Madeline picked up the rope and inspected it. "You would have fallen into the well if this was any worse."

Amberbirch touched the ragged threads that had burst from the braids. "Nothing short of a knife or fire would normally damage an elven rope." She looked at Springheart, eyes cold. "Come back to the grass and tell us exactly how this occurred."

Despite his protests that he was capable of moving on his own, Jode and Regis helped Springheart to the picnic area. Once settled with a plate of food and mug of wine, the elf gave them the facts. "I did nothing to disturb anyone, or anything, unless simply entering the well would have that effect. I put no more strain on the rope than I have in the past. This fraying of the strands... I don't remember anything happening that could have caused it." He looked to Regis as though for confirmation. Regis shrugged.

Amberbirch did not seem satisfied with the answer. Before she could interrogate Springheart, Madeline jumped in and asked, "Was all of it worth something?"

Springheart reached into his jacket and withdrew the notes he'd made. Handing them to Madeline, he took a long drink from the cup that Amberbirch had brought.

Madeline laid his notes beside the drawing that Regis had

done earlier. "I still feel like we are missing something," she said pensively. "I can sense a pattern here that is just out of my understanding." She stood away from the papers and glanced out over the stone bowl.

Regis stood beside her. "We thought to build a stand over the opening. Something that will allow us to see any pattern in the stones from the center."

Madeline shuddered at the thought of any of them returning to that well. "Not today. We'll come back when the sun is high. I'm not sure that Springheart would have survived that attack unless the sun was high and strong enough to warm him."

Jode joined them placing his arm around Madeline. "You think it was a purposeful attack?"

She looked up at him, pressing closer in his arms. "Yes. I think something caused that to happen."

"Are you sure that you have this word correct?" Amberbirch asked. "I cannot believe this was inscribed there."

Madeline turned to see their adviser holding the new sketch. She wanted to tell the woman to be less harsh with Springheart but knew that her understanding of elven manners wasn't strong enough to judge. "Does it mean something?" She tried to manage the hope that caught her breath at the thought that they may have a clue.

Amberbirch looked up. "Perhaps, but I will need to study this a little longer. The message I see has too many meanings to be helpful. Something is still missing," she said frowning her exasperation. Another glance at Springheart, the accusation clear on her face.

"I am sure Springheart was careful to be accurate with his work. Now that we have more information to analyze, we should return to the library," Madeline said. She bent to gather the plates and leftovers into a bundle. When Amberbirch told her to leave them for the servants, Madeline responded, "I will not send the servants out here alone. We may have made it more dangerous today."

The woman opened her mouth to argue, but seemed to think better of it. "As you wish."

Regis and Jode said they would walk the hills looking for a pattern in the stones before the party left. When Madeline stopped packing, and offered to join them, Jode said, "We will simply walk the rises to see if there is a possibility of an actual pattern rather than just uneven wear on the pavers. If so, we can return with the platform and more paper to investigate fully."

Madeline told them to hurry. "We are not leaving without you," she insisted.

THAT EVENING they were huddled around a table. The survey had revealed a pattern, still broken enough that Madeline couldn't determine meaning. So far it had not provided any clarity on the words engraved on the stones.

Madeline had arranged for the words to be copied several times. They each had an original, and there was a full set of sheets each representing a single stone. "If we had a computer, we could create a model and have the answer within minutes," she said. Seeing the confused looks on the faces around her, she continued, "It doesn't matter. We can return to the well tomorrow with equipment. Perhaps the pattern is more clear from the center. I find it hard to believe the pattern is really broken. A different view may show the remaining details."

Amberbirch moved the separate words around. "Surely we should be able to create a true representation. We have all of the elements."

Madeline tried not to take it as a criticism. She agreed with the woman after all. The sketches that Jode and Regis had made of the patterns they saw, allowed her to remove some of the words, but they still didn't make sense. "The words from within the well. Perhaps they give a hint on how to read the patterns."

"It is not always possible to know the real meaning of Elven messages," Amberbirch said. She pushed the papers into a different order.

Madeline bit back the words that rushed to her. They needed to stay positive, not worry about how difficult it could be. "The message must mean something. Why would someone carve these words simply to confuse us?"

Amberbirch didn't look up from the spread of notes. "Yes, it is about finding what they meant within the puzzle they set us. It is too easy to create any message that we want from the words. We need to know that we have the original message."

Madeline turned to Springheart, ignoring the woman's words. "What do you think? You've spent the afternoon sorting through them."

He laid out three more sheets of paper. "This is an ancient script. You are right, I think the words outside the well require a key. It may be that there are specific conditions, like the angle of the sun, or the season of the year, or something I have yet to think of. I've managed to divine three meanings." He pointed to the first sheet. "This says that the gate will be open until The Chosen One comes to seal it." He moved a second sheet closer. "This interpretation says that the gate can be sealed from our side if all of the conditions are met. And this final one, states that the one who can seal the gate will decipher the clues."

"Well that means I am not The Chosen One," Madeline said. "I didn't even know that there could be three different messages from the same words."

Springheart laughed. "It is not that the same words have three meanings in the same order. I took advice from the patterns we saw, and reordered the words until I could no longer find a meaning."

Madeline looked at the ten words Springheart had translated.

Then at the hundred separate words they still needed to under-stand. "We will need more time than we have to make this work." Knowing that some words could be read differently forward and backward, as well as at least three patterns they had determined, the number of possible meanings was too high to calculate.

She rested her elbows on the table and stared at the sheets of paper. Maybe there was a spell to bring the message forth. If there was, it would have to be deciphered by someone else.

Jode sat beside her and said, "Perhaps your role is to point the way, not to solve it yourself."

5

The next morning, after only a few hours' sleep, Madeline sat in the courtyard facing the rising sun. The direction Blu would come from. The direction hope would come from. It felt like they were grasping at the edge of the solution. Hints and clues appeared only to become puzzles of their own.

Amberbirch was doing her best, but the knowledge had been buried so deep in the library that it was a quest of its own to find it. And she was being so difficult with Springheart that Madeline found herself questioning everything that she thought was true. Afraid that some critical part of the answer was lost, Madeline spent most of her time double checking her own results.

She worried that there was no answer. Surely the elves would have found a way to close the gate by now. It didn't make any sense that they were content to simply fight a battle every time the gate opened.

The sun lifted from the top of the hills in the distance, bathing the world in warm light. Madeline tried to draw hope from the light, knowing that this despair she felt would never help them get to the solution and save the world.

She grunted a bitter laugh. How many movies had she watched and poked fun at because the hero would always emerge victorious against unspeakable odds? She needed a dose of that Hollywood brash hero. "Maybe I need a catch-phrase. Something to disarm the villain." And that was the real problem. Her villain was on the other side of the gate. She couldn't demoralize the minions, she couldn't pick them off one at a time, and she couldn't blow up the building and kill all the bad guys. By the time they came into reach, it would be too late.

Hunger took her attention away from contemplation. She'd been lucky enough to avoid morning sickness, so far. She'd happily trade morning sickness for a hint, if that's all the luck she was going to get.

She rose to join whoever was up for breakfast and then froze. Someone was standing in the corner. The shadow seemed to flicker. Madeline's heart stopped beating. She had no weapons, no magic. The courtyard was clear of anything she could throw, and her voice was frozen in her throat.

Had something made it through the gate early?

The shadow moved forward into the light. Amberbirch smiled and held out her hands. "You should be sleeping, Madeline."

Madeline's heart started beating again. Dizziness washed over her, and she staggered.

Amberbirch rushed forward to catch her. "What is wrong? Should I summon Jode?"

Allowing the elven woman to assist her to a seat, Madeline found her voice. "No. I'm fine. I was just startled. I didn't hear you arrive, and my imagination ran away with my sense."

Sitting beside her, Amberbirch placed her hand gently on Madeline's forehead. "You are cold. Let me get something to warm you. Some tea?"

Madeline waved away her concern. "I'll be fine in a moment. I thought I might be able to meditate my way to an answer. I guess I lost track of the world."

"And I stayed back hoping not to disturb you." She laughed gently. "We are a pair are we not?"

Madeline found her humor returning and laughed with Amberbirch, glad that the woman was in a positive mood this morning.

Amberbirch patted Madeline's hand. "You are worried that we will fail."

Feeling the doubts rise again, Madeline nodded, unwilling to voice the words.

"You have already found clues we have not been able to find in all of our research. I am sure you will succeed." Amberbirch smiled, but Madeline thought she heard doubt in the tone.

Telling herself that the doubt was all in her own mind, Madeline said, "I haven't found anything of use. I feel as though I have just clouded the issue more." She wanted to hear that Amberbirch had found the answer to the puzzle in the night. That The Chosen One had only to act, not to solve the riddles.

Amberbirch smiled reassurance. "I know it can feel that way. I feel that way sometimes, but do not lose sight of how much more we know. Today we will return to the gate. Your idea of a pattern will prove to be the final piece we need."

Madeline tried to buy into the optimism. It would help to see if there was a pattern, or even if there wasn't. Without a pattern, they would be sure that it was only a matter of making the right combination of the words. With a pattern... well it was the same, just with a few more points of reference.

"The platform is ready and the artisan also created a model. It is made of wooden tiles that can be raised or lowered individually." Amberbirch urged Madeline to rise and follow her to the dining hall. "With this, we can attach the various words and arrange them according to the pattern."

Madeline's mind started to run to the possibilities. She'd

wished for a computer, and suddenly this world's equivalent was created. She stood still and closed her eyes. "I wish for the answer to this riddle." *It can't hurt.* She opened her eyes and followed Amberbirch to breakfast.

THEY ARRIVED at the circle of stones just before noon. Amberbirch had stayed at the library with a copy of the words they had found. She would spend the day researching meanings.

The platform unfolded into a three-foot-high structure; the legs spanned the hole with room to spare. The builder had thought to place steps on each side, in case they disturbed something again. No one would be trapped. There was room for all four of them to stand or sit.

Madeline turned full circle, wondering if the new height would give her an answer. There was definitely a difference in the way the stones sat. It was subtle enough that walking would not show it if you weren't expecting it. The problem was it didn't actually form a pattern. If the new model was to be of any use, they needed a pattern.

She looked up. The sun would be at its high point soon. "We'll need to work fast. We should each take a quarter of the spiral. If a pattern emerges, we'll record it fast."

Jode placed his hand on her shoulder. "I think one of us should remain on guard. I have little skill in drawing, so I shall watch for threats."

"There's no one around, so there shouldn't be any danger," Madeline said.

Jode kissed the top of her head. "Danger can come more quickly than you think. I will still be of more use standing guard."

Regis handed paper to the others; the stones already drawn with the words added. All they would need to do was add shading. "A third of the spiral is not that much more than a quarter. It will be good to think we are protected from falling off the platform if we are engrossed in recording."

Madeline nodded, and then pointed to the circle of stones. "Look, it's started." The sun was picking out the small differences in the set of the stones. A pattern was emerging, stable and becoming more clear as the light moved to the top of its arc. "It's not going to be clear at midday, only as the sun approaches noon, and possibly shortly after. Quick, start sketching." She turned her attention away from Jode, trusting him to do his job.

The three stood back to back. Madeline heard faint scratches of charcoal on paper, and then nothing as her concentration narrowed only to the stones in her section of the path. It took moments for her to capture the pattern. The sun rose to the peak of noon, and Madeline saw the pattern disappear, then, as the sun started its descent, a new pattern grew. It was the negative of the original. Not new information, but confirmation.

Madeline smiled. They had achieved something.

"Everyone, run!" Jode's voice shattered her feeling of accomplishment. Her feet moved without her mind questioning. She ran to the far side of the stones. Noticing the others arriving near their supplies only as she stumbled to the edge. In her hand was the sheet of paper.

Her hair was whipping around her face, and a howling tore at her mind. It was filling her ears, but it seemed to be coming from inside her. There were no other sounds. Then it stopped. She stumbled because she'd been struggling to stand against the force of the wind. Along with the wind, the howling stopped, but there was a vacuum left, no sounds replaced it.

She started to ask what happened, but closed her mouth as the sight before her made it through her shock. The wind had toppled the platform, and the cloud of dust whirled in a tight funnel. The wind hadn't died, it was retreating into the well.

Jode took the papers she still clutched in her hands. He mouthed something, but his words were drowned out by the ringing in her ears. He drew her to the blanket and pressed her to sit. Regis and Springheart joined her, shaking their heads.

Holding his finger to his lips, Jode took a blank sheet and wrote, *can anyone hear me?* His lips moved as he pointed to the page.

Madeline shook her head noticing that Regis did the same. Springheart's mouth moved. His ears must have survived.

Jode wrote a second line. *It will likely pass. Are you otherwise hurt?*

Madeline shook her head and looked at Regis. He was rubbing his knee, but shook his head. It could have been a lot worse. One of them, or all of them, could have been falling into the hole. At least they had the pattern, at least they could reconstruct it. She hoped that this would lead them to some answers, not more questions.

6

That evening they sat under candlelight and stared at the wooden model. The artisan had done a great job of giving them the ability to manipulate it. The tiles were all arranged to match the pattern they had recorded earlier.

The words still made no sense.

"It feels as if we are looking at the pattern wrong," Regis said. "I don't know what it is, but the pattern does not look like a real pattern."

Madeline knew what he meant. Each tile that was raised, was a little different from the others. It was like they were trying to solve a jigsaw puzzle from the back. Multiple pieces fit together, but only the right ones produced the picture. The problem was, they didn't have the picture to help them know when they had it right.

"It's impossible," she said. "I don't know what I can do. We've tried everything but magic, and I don't have magic."

Springheart leaned in. "There are others who have magic. Is there something you would like us to try?"

That was something Madeline hadn't considered. "I am used

to doing things myself. Before I just knew what to do — or I reacted instinctively. I don't know how to tell you what needs to be done."

The revelation sat her back on her heels. The others were waiting for her to accept the offer, or direct the magic. They all had different magic. Regis could use his over distances that most people would consider impossible. He could create charms and do magic directly with his mind. The problem was her babies had co-opted some of his magic the way they'd stolen hers. Spring-heart had the same magic as all the elves; both he and Amber-birch were able to heal others. He'd healed Regis' twisted knee that afternoon. Jode didn't have any magic.

Her own power was prescience. She'd learned to use ribbon magic from Blu, and she could enter a trance and bring up visions. None of their talents overlapped.

She felt the pressure of their gazes and shook herself out of her fog. "I'll have to think about it. It's something new." She smiled up at them and tried to be kind. "It might be better to think this through alone."

Jode looked at her, frowning. He knew her well enough to hear the lie, but he nodded and led the others away. Madeline waited until she was sure he wasn't coming back to get the truth out of her. Then she wrapped herself in a woolen shawl and curled up on a sofa.

She needed to get her magic back. The babies hadn't used the power, so they didn't need it. She wished she knew why they'd taken it. Callisra said she'd never heard of it happening before.

Madeline placed her hands on her rounded belly. "What are you up to you little scamps?" She didn't expect an answer, but felt disappointment when it didn't come.

She relaxed and thought of the peaceful place she would retreat to in her mind when trying a difficult spell. Imagining the sun warming her skin, she shucked the shawl. The sound of waves filled her mind, the feeling of the fine grit of the sand beneath her toes helped her to slide into the trance.

She held onto the feeling gently, knowing that if she tried too hard, it would slip away. Now that she was in the place, she didn't know what it meant. Was she accessing the magic? It felt as though she was really on the beach, but that could be her imagination taking over.

She looked around. It was almost exactly as she remembered it. The only difference was a small hut on the edge of the trees. She couldn't remember it being there before, but she'd rarely stayed long enough to notice much. Madeline walked toward the hut, curious as to why she needed a residence in her imaginary place.

As she neared, she heard giggling. There were children there. Her children?

Madeline hurried. If her children were in that hut, maybe she could talk to them. It made no sense, but she didn't care. The giggling got louder as she approached. Running around the hut, Madeline couldn't find a door. There was no way in. There was a window high up, so she could look in if she could pull herself up.

Reaching for the sill, Madeline was able to grasp it, but needed to raise herself a foot to look in. She could feel the rough wood beneath her fingers. As she noticed, the feeling faded. Panic froze her as the sound of the waves dimmed. She let go of the window frame and calmed her thoughts. The sounds strengthened, including the giggles. Taking a deep breath, Madeline pulled herself up to look in the window.

She saw two children about three years old, red hair hanging in ringlets, a boy, and a girl. They tossed glowing ribbons between them. Madeline watched the ribbons drift toward her. It was her magic. The children stopped giggling and turned to watch the ribbons. They saw her and disappeared.

Madeline fell to the sand as the hut disappeared, then to the ground when the sand disappeared. She opened her eyes to see the library around her. Cold stone under her as she lay on the floor, having fallen from the couch.

"Damn, damn, damn." Madeline struggled to untangle herself from the shawl.

Jode rushed into the room. "What has happened?" He had his sword ready to attack.

Madeline giggled, an echo of the sound of the children. "Nothing… well nothing here." She let him help her onto the couch; he handed her a glass of water from the table.

"Tell me where you have been and what happened," he said, joining her on the couch.

Madeline related her journey. "If I could have talked to them, or kept their attention just for a moment longer, I could have my magic back. That would solve our problem."

He hugged her. "Are you sure this vision was truthful?"

Madeline nestled into his embrace. "Yes, I am. There was something about the encounter. It felt like I'd already seen them playing. They were so happy."

"A boy and a girl." He kissed the top of her head. "They already have my heart."

She laughed. "They have my heart too, and my magic."

"I'm sure you will find a solution in time."

Madeline appreciated his confidence but didn't share it. "We have to get the magic back."

"What do you mean?" Amberbirch asked from the door. "I am sorry to intrude, but did you say you have magic, but it has been taken?"

Madeline explained what had happened, from the children taking her magic to the vision she'd just experienced.

Amberbirch listened carefully then said, "I have only heard of this happening once. A very long time ago. When that happened, the mother did regain her powers after the child was born."

Madeline slumped. She'd been hoping Amberbirch had a solution. "We need it before I give birth in six months."

Amberbirch nodded. "That would be good. It may be that there is a healing charm to resolve this. I will investigate. Now you must rest. This is not good for the babies."

7

The next morning, Madeline returned to the wooden model after eating a full breakfast. Having told Amberbirch about her magic, she'd felt a lift of the burden of solving one of the many problems on her list. Up to now, all she'd been told was that no one knew of this happening before, but Amberbirch had been confident that there was a solution.

She stepped into the room that they were using as a war room and saw Amberbirch talking to an elf who was so old and shrunken that Madeline couldn't tell if it was a man or a woman.

Amberbirch looked up, alerted to Madeline's presence by the other elf. "Madeline, we have been waiting for you. This is our oldest healer, Blackoak. He would like to examine you to see if we can convince the babies to return you power, at least for a while."

Blackoak bowed and held out a wrinkled hand to Madeline. "It will be my honor to help."

Madeline smiled, hoping that it would work, desperate for it to be the answer, but still terrified that it would harm her children to take the magic back. "It is my honor to meet you,

Blackoak. I am yours to examine." She couldn't believe examination would hurt.

Blackoak patted her hand and drew her to the couch. "Lie here, my dear," he said in a quiet but firm voice. "I will only need to place my hands on your belly to seek out these mischievous children. You know, we believe that the personality is formed immediately on conception. You will have your hands full with these two as they grow."

Madeline lay back, the healer's confidence giving her a sense of comfort. "I was a bit of a challenge to my parents, so I guess it's only fair that my children challenge me."

Blackoak chuckled. He lifted her shirt to allow his hands to touch her skin. Madeline felt embarrassed at the sight of the rounded bump. It was growing much faster than she expected. But then, she'd never known anyone who carried twins, so perhaps two children needed twice the room. She suddenly realized that they would be little humans now, not just blobs. It wouldn't be long before she would feel them move.

Blackoak's voice broke her daydream. "Would you like to see what I see?"

"Yes, please," Madeline said. "Perhaps we can get Jode here?" She felt like it was her first ultrasound. If she would see the babies, it should be simple for them to link Jode in and let him see them too.

Blackoak glanced at Amberbirch. The elven woman was outside of Madeline's line of sight, so she didn't see the reaction. Blackoak shook his head. "Let us do this with only you and me. I do not wish to startle the babies."

Madeline felt disappointed not to be able to share the experience. Surely the children would want to meet their father. Amberbirch patted her hand, and Madeline remembered why they were trying to contact the babies. If they were successful, she could show Jode herself. She nodded and focused her mind on observing how Blackoak made the connection.

She saw a silver ribbon of magic shine against absolute dark. The magic felt like Blackoak. Madeline had expected to find an avatar of the elf waiting, but it seemed like she was alone, and could only observe. She wanted so much to ask questions, to find out if the children were healthy, to introduce herself.

The path spiraled down to a center point, giving her a sense of direction and position. Madeline's spirit glided forward, and at the second turn in the path, she saw two bright lights at the end. One light was orange the other blue, then they flickered and changed to red and green. "Do not worry," Blackoak's voice came into her mind. "They are healthy and active."

"Are you going to talk to them?" she thought the question.

No answer came.

As she approached the two lights, Madeline felt joy and excitement rise. Another turn of the spiral and she would be there. She glided the last few feet and suddenly found herself on the couch in her own body, staring up at Amberbirch and Blackoak.

"Why…" she started to ask.

"Do not worry," Blackoak said. "I have the knowledge I sought. We will have your magic back in a few minutes."

"Wait," Madeline said sitting up. "I need to know exactly what you are going to do."

Amberbirch frowned. "We cannot allow you to learn all of our magic, Madeline. There are some secrets that must be kept to the elves."

Madeline wasn't surprised at the answer, and shook her head. "No, I don't need to know the magic. I just need to understand what you are going to do." The fear that something would hurt the babies overrode every other consideration.

Amberbirch started to answer. Blackoak held up a hand to stop her. "Your babies are safe and will remain so. But would you sell the whole world to save these two?"

She hadn't expected to have to answer that question. Until

now it had been an intellectual choice. Of course, she wouldn't sacrifice the world for one or two lives. Even after her vision of the two children in the hut, she would have said that. After all, that could have been wishful thinking. Now that she had seen those lights, and knew that they were her children, she wasn't so sure. Cartref had survived this event before. It was only a fear that this time it would be so much worse, that the people of the whole of the world would die. It felt unreal that something so devastating could happen.

"I cannot say," she finally answered. "That is something no one can know unless they are faced with the choice. If I asked you the same, would you sacrifice the entire elven race to save the world? Would you be able to answer?"

Something flashed in Amberbirch's eyes before she stepped away. Blackoak flicked a glance at the other woman before answering. "You are correct. We can only hope that we will do the right thing. We cannot know until the moment is upon us. But the elves have made this choice many times. And we have always chosen Cartref."

Feeling chastened, Madeline nodded. "This time, Jode needs to be here. Please bring him, Amberbirch. We will both hear what you need to do before it happens."

Amberbirch hurried to obey Madeline's request. While Madeline and Blackoak were alone, she asked him, "Can you tell why they took my magic?"

"We cannot know why, just that they are healthy," Blackoak responded. "When you are finished with sealing the gate, perhaps you can visit with my mother. She is the oldest of us and as such has more wisdom and knowledge than I. She may have an answer, if you are still interested."

When Jode arrived, Blackoak explained that he would return to the children and take the power back. "They will not be happy, but I have more power than they do. They cannot use your power, Madeline. It is only a toy to them. It will not hurt them to give it up, but as I said, they will not be happy. It is possible you will feel their displeasure."

Madeline looked at Jode who took her hand and held it tightly. "Are you sure it will not harm them?" Blackoak smiled at her and gave a quick nod. She sighed. "I've had a pretty easy pregnancy so far. Let's get on with it."

She arranged herself in Jode's embrace and closed her eyes. Blackoak placed his hands on her belly again, this time she was not invited to join him. Where the elf's hands touched, she felt warmth. It was reassuring. She could feel Jode's arms around her, holding her safe. He seemed to have no worries. She knew that part of what the elf was doing had nothing to do with reaching the children, he was doing something to calm the parents. It worried her, but she couldn't hold onto any of the concern. As she thought of the risk, the feeling slipped away.

All was still for a moment. Madeline opened her eyes. She saw Blackoak's bald head bent over her, his forehead touching her belly, hands to either side. She heard a quiet muttering, as if he was trying to communicate with the babies.

Suddenly, Madeline felt a flush of heat travel from her center to her extremities. Sweat broke out all over her skin and then dried as her body cooled. Something was different. She felt whole.

Blackoak looked up, drawing away. "Can you feel your magic?"

Madeline cast her senses out and grinned at the feeling of connection. "Yes, it's back."

Jode kissed her and patted the bump. Suddenly Madeline felt a squirm of movement under his hand. Then a swift elbow to her ribs.

She winced and then laughed. "You were right. They are not happy with me."

8

The next morning, Madeline knew she had to return to the gate. Having her magic back wasn't going to be of help unless she took it to the source. She'd rested all afternoon yesterday. It meant that she couldn't find sleep when it came time. As soon as Jode had fallen asleep, she had risen and spent the night preparing. The wind was her biggest worry. It seemed to be stronger the second time. If that happened again, they might lose someone.

She didn't need to be in the center to perform the spell she had planned. She couldn't rely on proximity being the trigger for the wind, based on only the two events. On the table, ready to be packed were three ropes, the wooden model, and a blanket.

"What are you planning?" Jode asked as he joined her. "You didn't get much sleep."

Madeline smiled. "I thought you were too far gone to notice."

"I always know when you leave our bed. I also know that sometimes it is better to let you leave."

She loved the way he seemed to know her. In her time on Cartref, she's only had a few months to be at peace, so they hadn't tested their ability to live as a married couple. When this was over, they would only have a few months before the children arrived. She promised herself that she would commit her energy to keeping their family happy and together.

"We have to go back," she said. "I need to see what has happened on the site."

"You plan to recall the events of the past, as you did with the Choi?" Jode asked.

Madeline nodded. "I think it might take a lot of energy to go back far enough into the past."

"Are you sure you have that energy?" He looked at her critically. "You look pale, and tired."

"I have to have it." She wished she had a choice. There was no time for her to rest. "I'm not a delicate flower."

He reached for her and drew her into a hug. "It is my job to worry about you. And you are not getting enough rest. You not only look pale; you feel like you are fading away. Pregnant women need to take care of themselves."

Madeline rubbed her cheeks to bring some color to them. "Is that better?" she asked.

He sighed and let her go. "No, but it will do."

She wanted to pull him into their bed and sleep for hours. Instead, she said, "I'm fine, Jode. Go wake the others, and I'll get the servants to bring breakfast."

AT THE SITE of the gate, Madeline spread the blanket and laid the model in the center. She checked and adjusted it, so the orientation was identical to the stone version. Then she laid papers around it with charcoal ready beside each.

"Is there something we can do to help?" Regis asked.

Madeline looked up from her task. "I'm just trying to make sure this is ready for me to make notes as soon as I come out of the trance. I don't want to lose anything I might find."

He nodded. "Perhaps Springheart and I can ensure the model

is correctly set to the pattern. Then Jode can attach the ropes to your body. I think we all would prefer to spend as little time as necessary here."

Madeline glanced at the stone circle and then at the model. "Good idea. I don't know how long I'll be in the trance, but I want to go as far back as I can."

Springheart joined Regis in fussing with the model. Madeline walked to where Jode was checking each inch of the ropes. She sat beside him. "I checked it this morning," she said. "It's all good."

He kept running the ropes between his fingers. "Yes, and the rope was whole when Springheart entered the well. I will feel better when I have checked it. How close will you get to the center?"

Madeline glanced at the hole; she could just see the edge of it from where she sat. The bowl was very shallow, just enough to make the person standing on the edge feel drawn to the center. "I'll stand on the edge here. If I need to go further, I'll only go as far as I have to." She shivered. "It feels like the well is developing a malevolent spirit. It must be my imagination."

When she turned back to Jode, he was staring at her. "It may not be your imagination. Take care."

She took the rope he'd finished examining, wound it around her chest, and tied a loose knot. "Pull me back if I get more than two turns in."

He nodded and finished checking the ropes in silence. In the quiet, Madeline reviewed the process she'd used to trace the Choi. She'd used the report of the aftermath of the fire to drive the spell. If she went as far back as the last battle, she may not have the energy to sustain the vision. She decided to just let the vision run back from the events of their first visit, a little more than two months ago. It might take some time, but at least she would be in control. And if she had to withdraw, she'd have another starting point for the next time.

Springheart and Regis confirmed that they were finished.

Jode picked up the two ropes and they stood together at the edge of the stone circle. Jode corrected the knot she'd tied, and then attached the other two ropes. He handed the ends to Regis and Springheart before nodding to Madeline. "Go now before I cannot restrain myself from stopping you."

Madeline touched the ropes, and then stepped onto the stone. She closed her eyes and remembered the first time she'd seen the circle. Amberbirch had stepped onto the first stone to explain the words and the process.

The scene sprang to life in Madeline's mind. Then the sky spun, and Amberbirch disappeared. The seasons flicked by, casting rain and sun and the occasional coating of snow. Within a few minutes, Madeline thought that she'd seen more than fifty years pass. At this pace, she would be seeing the last battle soon. Despite her worries, the spell wasn't drawing energy, so Madeline allowed the years to pass quickly.

The battle flickered in her vision, a century and a half had passed. It could only have taken a few days to complete, otherwise she would have seen more than just some sense of noise, blood, and fear. The vision slowed its pace without her taking any action. Then it came to a stop. Three elves were standing at the edge of the well, but she could see them as clearly as if they were in front of her. The elves all wore gray robes with hoods, so she couldn't see any distinguishing features. In fact, she was unsure if they were male or female. The only difference was that one was larger. The other two elves looked to the larger one for answers.

Madeline leaned closer as if it made a difference to being able to hear. Her body was conscious that the ropes tightened and she relaxed.

Willing the conversation to come to her, Madeline started to hear words.

"Now that you know the message below, you do not need to go there again."

"Master, that is the first test, what is the second?" one of the smaller elves asked.

"Do you not retain anything the master tells us?" The second elf was definitely a woman – and annoyed. "There are three tests. We have just passed the first, which was to find the hidden message. The next test is to solve the riddle of the words outside the well. Then the last test will reveal the message."

The master held up a hand and shook his head. "Treat each other with respect. The elders left this as a tool for us to end this scourge of invasion. They wanted us to earn it, and we must work together to learn."

The first elf bowed and started to walk away. Why did the elves stop training new students on the message? These two were definitely being trained for some purpose.

Then the world spun again, and years peeled by at a pace that made Madeline stagger to retain her balance. Then everything suddenly came to a stop.

No one stood in the circle. The stones were different. They were not newer, but they seemed less settled somehow. Madeline knew that she should be able to see this clue, but she wasn't able to understand anything that would help.

Suddenly the stones started to move. Only the stones that formed the pattern they'd recorded at the rise of the sun. They rose and shifted position. The stones rose in seven concentric circles, each broken at the point where the spiral turned. Then each circle moved independently. The closest circle turned clockwise, the second counterclockwise, the third clockwise. The pattern continued to the center. Each circle moved one position over. Then settled back.

This couldn't have happened without someone casting a spell. Why would someone change the pattern and obscure the solution? She spun to try to catch the perpetrator and saw to her right, standing on the tenth stone, a tall creature, cloaked in crimson robes. It looked at her and she recognized it as a Scree. It rubbed its hands together and Madeline saw clouds of chalk blow away in the breeze.

Then the ropes tightened and drew her away from the circle and back to the present.

She stumbled back to the blanket. The three men were hauling on the ropes as if she'd been about to disappear down the well.

"Stop, I'm fine," she yelled as she tripped and landed on her butt.

Jode rushed to her side. "The wind came again, and we could not see you." He ran his hands over her body. "Are you sure you are not hurt?"

She took his hands in hers and squeezed, hoping to reassure him. "I am. I didn't know about the wind. I must have been too deep in the trance." Madeline wiggled out of his embrace and reached for the model. "The stones aren't the kind of pattern we thought." She told them what she'd seen.

"Why would the Scree want to keep the gate open," Regis asked. "In fact, if there is a solution, why wouldn't the elves have just sealed the gate as soon as they found it?"

Springheart looked over the model, his fingers tracing the original positions of the stones. "It is possible that the solution must be used when the gate is open. If the Scree changed the position, it is possible that the stones were moved more than three hundred years ago."

Madeline untied the knots holding the ropes to her. "Let's take it all back to the library. We'll get the artisans to make the changes I saw. Maybe we'll have our answer right away." And I will find out why the elves stopped training people.

9

*A*t the library, Amberbirch sent for the artisans and then helped Madeline rearrange the paper version of the stones. "If the original position of the stones provides us with an answer, we can look forward to a long and peaceful life. You will be a hero to all of the people of Cartref."

Jode agreed, looking proud of her.

Madeline shook her head. "I'm not a hero. I just want to settle down and have my family safe around me." She laughed. "I would never have said that before coming here. I saw something else. I don't understand what it means, but I saw an elf teaching two students about the message at the gate."

Amberbirch rearranged the papers on the table before finally looking at Madeline. "Yes, there was a time when the knowledge was passed through the generations."

Annoyed that Amberbirch didn't just give her the information, Madeline asked, "Why did they stop?"

Amberbirch walked to the window and glanced out before answering. It was as if she had to gather her thoughts, but Madeline had an ugly suspicion that she was gathering her lies. Turning back to them, Amberbirch said, "I should have mentioned it before, but I thought it had no value now that The Chosen was finally here. But your vision of the stones moving brings new meaning to the tale."

"What tale?" Madeline's tone was abrupt, and she regretted it as soon as the words were out of her mouth.

"We thought that information had been lost in the telling. But now we know that the message was changed." Amberbirch pulled her robe closer around her, for warmth, or comfort. "Between one generation and the next, the stones were moved. The students were unable to decipher the message. The teacher could not find what he knew was there. We stopped teaching and prepared for the next battle."

"Is there anything else that doesn't seem important?" Madeline asked.

Amberbirch gave a bitter laugh. "Many things, but I'm sure you don't want to spend time hearing every rumor and guess we've had in the last hundred years."

Madeline wished she could, but had to trust that Amberbirch would be more alert to rumors that might be pertinent. "Let's get back to what we were doing."

Regis and Springheart joined them, leaning over the scraps of paper. "It is hard to see how the spiral works with this paper version," Regis said. "If we could make it circular, maybe it would work, but I find it hard to keep track of where the original stones were as I try to move them. How long will it take to get the model changed?"

Amberbirch tried to move the papers into a better simulation of the stone spiral. She gave up as the pieces moved in a slight breeze. "Tomorrow morning. But is it wise to wait? We have the answer here if we can create a better model."

Madeline rubbed her temples to ease the beginning of a headache. The papers around her kept shifting. If they weighed them down, then moving them was too difficult. "No, let's wait for the model."

Regis looked at the pages. "If we laid them out in order... does it need to be a spiral?"

"Yes," Springheart answered. "It may be that the position of the word in relation to the others is important. I agree with Madeline, we should wait for the model to be ready."

After collecting the papers, the group separated to fill their time with other activities. Madeline stayed in the library, deciding to look through some of the histories for something to give her a flavor of the world the last time the gate opened.

She walked along the shelves holding her translation sheet in front of her. The titles were not designed to intrigue anyone looking for light reading. Everything was the history of one family or another, one hero or another. The latter seemed interesting until she opened the first. It started with the detailed history of the lineage of the hero. Two hundred pages in, the record was still four generations removed from the subject of the history.

One small book tucked into the last place on the shelf looked promising. It wasn't elvish, it was Mariai, the people of The City.

Madeline curled up on the couch and laid the translation sheet over the first page. *The tale of Mascura and the elven puzzle.* She followed the story of a Mariai adventurer who stole some gold from a group of elves. When they caught him, and the gold was returned, the elves applied an interesting test to determine his punishment. If Mascura could solve the riddle, he would be set free. If he could not, he would have to serve ten years as a slave.

As she read, Madeline started working out the puzzle. The Mariai had to decipher a statement and complete the action it described. The words seemed to be straight forward, directing Mascura to a specific tree in the local forest. There would be an object there that he needed to return to the family as proof of his success.

The first few pages should have been enough to tell the story, but it unfolded into a more complex tale. Mascura had discovered a trick in the message. The plain reading was clearly to head northwest and find a willow. He found a secondary meaning that would lead him northeast to an oak. Eventually Mascura was successful in deciding which interpretation was correct.

Madeline tried to follow the logic that he used, but it included some knowledge of elves that was unstated. The moral was clearly laid out. If you are foolish enough to steal from elves, do not be foolish enough to think the reparation would be simple.

She closed the book and picked up Regis' original drawing. Knowing that the stones had been moved was a relief, but she already knew that the meanings could be subtly different depending on location. They wouldn't get a second chance to solve this riddle.

Would the elves have created a clear message, or was there going to be multiple meanings? And if there were, Madeline wondered how they would know which to pick.

10

Springheart looked at the original drawing of the stones. He'd marked the stones that had been moved, and the direction of movement. On another sheet of paper, he had carefully redrawn the stones and added the words on those that hadn't been moved. If he could complete the drawing, they could get a head start on understanding the instructions. More than two months of unsuccessful research had stretched his temper further than any event in his life up to now.

And this was not helping. He scratched out another error. Keeping track of the words that moved and their direction was difficult to say the least. The light was fading. He rubbed his eyes, but it didn't help clear the fuzziness of the characters on the paper.

"I thought you agreed that we should wait for the model," Regis said, placing a mug of wine on the table, and then a full jug. "It won't help for you to go blind."

Springheart piled the papers on the side before taking a sip of the wine. "I couldn't settle so I thought I would try, but it is as if the damn thing is cursed to be difficult to solve."

Regis laughed. "I've heard it said that an elf would obscure the cure for his own death. Your culture is to create ambiguity and confusion. I am surprised that it was a Scree who moved the stones."

Springheart couldn't take offense since Regis was only saying what the elven elders taught them. "How are you able to relax so easily?"

"Is there any benefit in getting upset? Will it help to solve this puzzle?" Regis drained his cup and then refilled it from the jug. "I have no special talents, or none beyond what others can bring. I try to be of assistance, but we know I am only here because I cannot be trusted to go to the Summer Lands without escort."

Springheart sipped his own wine before speaking. He knew that Regis didn't truly believe his words. "If that were true, you could have left with Simon and Callisra when they departed for the Summer Lands."

"Yes, but I wasn't asked to join them," Regis replied. "I am not even worth getting rid of quickly."

Springheart slapped Regis on his knee. "You have worth my friend, and you know it. I would have fallen to my death in that well without you. Madeline would not have this drawing if you hadn't created it."

Regis waved off the praise. "The only thing that I had of value was my far casting magic. That is still in the possession of Madeline's unborn troublemakers. With that magic, I could reach out to others who may have knowledge we need. Without it, even my ability to scry is limited."

It was a good point Springheart conceded. There may not be many people who could give advice, but they lived at a distance. If Regis had the ability to contact them, then a discussion might find a solution. Springheart had no doubt that a solution existed. "Perhaps we should try to bring your magic back to you."

Regis laughed. "Even if Madeline agreed, they will not be so easy to trick a second time."

"Do not be so sure that is the only way." Springheart stretched

54

out the kinks in his back. "I know of a spell that will return what is lost. Perhaps that will work."

"And how do you plan to get Madeline to agree. I will not attempt anything that disturbs her children." Regis was clearly trying to sound like he didn't care, but Springheart heard the yearning in his friend's voice.

It was hard to imagine what losing your magic would feel like, but if Regis was any example, it must be like losing a limb. Something you could learn to do without, but you would always miss the ability it gave you.

"Leave it to me." He left Regis at the table, refilled cup in hand, while he went to talk to Madeline.

It took a little longer than anticipated, but, when Madeline was convinced that the spell would not harm her children, she agreed to let Springheart try. He left Amberbirch monitoring Madeline and returned to Regis.

"I need something from you to make this work," he said. "It is in the nature of an exchange. We will provide the children with a new amusement and they will release your magic."

Regis looked doubtful. "I don't understand why they need entertaining. It is not normal for unborn children to be aware. Children don't require amusement until long after they are born."

Springheart agreed with Regis' assessment and worried at the precocity of these children. But there was nothing to be gained from discussing the possible reasons, and Regis could do more of value with his power than they could. That had been the final argument to Madeline. "I am sure we will learn the reason when they are born, but, for now, you can have your magic back in exchange for another amusement."

Regis lounged back on his seat. "I suppose we cannot offer a bright shiny object to them?"

Laughing, Springheart shook his head. "It cannot be a material object. You will have to offer a skill or a talent."

"Hmm, I see the challenge I face. What would I prefer to lose, my ability to sing, or my ability to reach out to people who may help solve the problem?"

Springheart let Regis think through the options as he laid out a drawing of the spell he would use. The transfer would be simple. He'd seen it done on adults, temporarily transferring skills between them, then back. The babies may not be born, but they were definitely conscious of their skills and needs. "It can be something you can learn again, or perhaps you will be able to convince them to return your talent in the future."

"I will offer my ability to draw," Regis said. "It has already served a purpose."

Springheart moved the wine jug and mugs aside to place the paper in the center. "Amberbirch will sever the connection if there is any detriment to the children. We will use this image as a portal to them. I will keep you grounded here through my touch. You will be the one who negotiates. When you are done, the spell will end naturally."

"Will you be able to hear what is happening?" Regis asked, his hand hovering over the drawing of a door. "Will I be alone?"

"You cannot take anyone with you," Springheart answered. "We cannot risk that they will steal other magic. Madeline was clear about that. She worries about them having power and no discretion." He placed his hand on Regis' shoulder. "When you are ready, put your hand on the picture, and imagine the infants that Madeline described seeing in the hut."

Springheart watched as Regis placed his hand flat on the paper, covering the drawing. His friend relaxed and closed his eyes. There was nothing to observe while the spell was in effect.

THE LIGHT of the fire faded into embers and Springheart itched to move from his position. The spell had been in effect for over an hour. Jode had reported that the babies were healthy, but quiet, shortly after Regis had entered the trance.

Suddenly, Regis jerked from Springheart's touch and took in a deep, ragged breath.

"It's done," he said. "I have my magic back and they have none."

Springheart felt more relief than he'd expected. When they had sealed the gate, as surely they must be on the verge of doing, he would suggest that Madeline take advantage of the elven healers to understand why this was happening. "Good, I'm sure that you can learn to draw as well as you did before."

Regis shook his head. "It was not that simple. They are canny children. I have agreed to protect them when they are born. My life is going to be much more unsettled than I expected." He laughed. "Arabela may be happier that I am not going to be living with her. It may make it easier to forgive me."

11

*T*he next morning, Madeline waited for delivery of the new model. Optimistic that this would be, if not the answer, a huge step forward. She paced the room, checking the path from the village through the window every few seconds.

"They will be here soon," Amberbirch said from her position at the table. "Come and help me to return all of these books to the shelves, so that we have the whole table cleared for work."

Madeline joined the elf and picked up a few books. "I read something yesterday about how elves tend to obscure answers to their riddles. Do you think that the words of the stones will be clear, or will we have to pick a meaning?"

Amberbirch looked at Madeline, a frown on her face. "I can only hope that the creators of this gate wanted us to seal it."

Madeline let the subject go; they would know soon enough what the words meant. "Why did someone build the gate?"

"To mark the place of danger," Amberbirch replied as she returned a book to the highest shelf. "They did not build the gate so much as mark the well. The spiral of words and the stones lining the well are much less ancient than the well itself."

That surprised Madeline, if the stones lining the well were a new addition, how had they been laid? "It must have been diffi-cult to place the stones inside the well with that wind rising."

Amberbirch reached for another book. "The wind was a surprise to me. It must be something that happens as the time of the invasion approaches."

Madeline stifled a look of surprise. This was the first time Amberbirch had volunteered a lack of knowledge. "None of the histories, or songs, mentioned it?"

"Despite our efforts, the songs have become useless children's rhymes. You must have noticed that the histories focus on the battle, rather than the efforts to prevent it." She finished placing books on the table and glanced out of the window. "I seem to share your impatience. It is frustrating to keep checking the window without seeing the wagon approach, but it does feel as though I am doing something." She turned away from the window and faced Madeline.

"It almost as satisfying to tell you that watching won't bring them sooner." Madeline laughed. "Tell me more about how they laid the stones inside. Even without the wind, how did they get the stones to adhere long enough to set?"

Amberbirch settled on a couch before answering. Her brow furrowed as though she was trying to bring up the memory. "I am not versed in stonework, but if I remember my research, the stones in the well were built outside and then inserted. The ones on the top held the arrangement in place until the mortar set."

Madeline tried to picture the work, but imagining the well brought back the feeling of the wind and dust. "Is there any possibility that the stones were placed in the wrong order?"

"No, that would have been checked a thousand times, I'm sure." Amberbirch motioned Madeline to join her. "How are the children?"

When Madeline's friends who'd had babies couldn't talk about anything but their offspring, it had bored her to the edge of screaming. It was part of the reason she drifted away from them.

Now that she bore her own twins, she understood how hard it was to not gush. "They are lively now. It's like they have just found a new toy – my body." She rubbed the side where she'd just received a sharp jab.

The elven woman smiled. "Twins are a rare thing for the elves. Will you allow our healers to assist you through the delivery?"

"It will be long after we are done here," Madeline said. "I yearn to have them born in my home. If I stay here, it will be a very long time before I can get home."

Amberbirch glanced away and then turned back to Madeline, pain in her eyes. "At least allow them to examine you. They may be able to advise you on how to make the birth as easy as possible."

The window was too high for Madeline to see through from her position on the couch, but she remembered she had her powers back. As she answered, Madeline sent her senses toward the elven village. "I agreed to let Blackoak's mother examine me." There was no traffic on the path from the village to the library.

"Blackoak's mother?" Amberbirch sat up quickly. "She passed three years ago."

Madeline had been about to mention that the model was not in transit when the words sunk in. "He said she might be able to explain why they took the magic."

Amberbirch patted Madeline's hand. "He misses her. I didn't realize how much. Thank you for telling me about this. I will have someone talk to him and help him through his grief."

He had seemed so sure, but Madeline handled enough estate files to know how grief could change the way someone looked at the world. She let the subject go. "I think we should send Spring-heart to the village. I don't think the model is on the way."

Amberbirch rose and gave Madeline a tiny bow. "There must be a problem with the design. You rest, I'll ask Springheart to check."

Madeline shook her head and rose. "I'll come along. If we are not getting the model, I would like us to get our ideas on the table. We've done all the research I think we can."

She followed Amberbirch to the grounds of the library. The others were practicing with their weapons and talking. Amberbirch sent one of the servants to the village to check on the model makers so that Springheart could join the conversation.

After they went through their combined understanding of the gate, Madeline felt her optimism slip away. There was no insight hidden between the cracks. They were stuck with waiting for the model and researching.

WHEN THE MODEL ARRIVED, they crowded around it. The makers had been instructed to create the ability to move the pieces. They had returned the model with the replica stones in their current positions. With everyone carefully checking her movements, Madeline duplicated the changes she'd seen the Scree make.

"The masons have gone to the gate to reposition the stones," Amberbirch said.

Shocked, Madeline looked up from the model. "That's too dangerous. Who told them to do it?"

Amberbirch straightened. "I did. I thought it would be better that the stones returned to their original positions. It would make it easier to understand the message."

"But the wind, the dust…" Madeline tried to keep panic from her voice.

Amberbirch waved the concern away. "They are masons. It will be done quickly, and I told them to make sure they were tethered. It will be fine."

Her tone didn't leave room for argument. Madeline realized that the damage, if there was any, had been done. She turned her attention back to the model. With the stones in the new positions, Madeline hoped that the message would be clear. Springheart and Amberbirch wrote out the message forward and back and sat together deciphering it. Madeline slumped in her chair, realizing the stupidity of her assumption. She'd been told that the words had different meanings depending on where they were in relationship to the words around them. Of course, having the words spelled out wouldn't result in an answer.

"You need to eat, my dear." Jode took her arm. "Watching will not make it go faster. In fact, I fear watching will place too much pressure on them and perhaps cause mistakes."

Regis joined them and tried to make Madeline feel better about the delay. "We haven't read all of the books in the library. I know it feels like it, but how about we make a list of those we still need to review?"

Madeline noticed that Jode was smiling, and she realized they were trying to placate her frustration. "Fine, but I can't promise not to be annoyed at the wait." She followed them to the shelves and started shuffling the books she'd read into one pile.

After a few minutes, there were only six books left. All of the other books that were about the gate and the history of the passage had been read by at least two of them. The remaining books were bound in leather and two were very slim volumes. *The Heroes of the Gate, a list of honor. The invader species,* and *the makers of the path.* "These might help Springheart and Amberbirch," Madeline said. "Perhaps the names of the people will have some impact on the meaning of the words. God knows it seems like everything else does."

Regis set them aside. "I'll take them in a minute." He pulled down the other three books. "These all seem to be variations on the information we already have."

Madeline took the thickest book and placed it on the table. Opening it to the center, she placed her translation sheet on it and read, "On the third day of meditation, Lightwillow heard the message of the gate and ran to warn the people to bring the army."

Regis placed his hand on the page. "I have some bad news, or perhaps it is good news too late."

Madeline looked up at him. "What is it?"

Turning the book around to face him, he said, "Read what you see now."

Madeline didn't understand why he was making it so difficult. "On the third—"

"No, read the book as though it were not upside down." He pointed to the top of the book.

Madeline frowned but turned her attention to the translation. "We were caught unaware by the wind that rose from the well. It brought forth a foul miasma of black motes. We would learn that on the final day, these motes would be the new invaders." She looked up at Regis and Jode, feeling ice crawling up her spine. "Oh shit. We've been reading the books the wrong way?"

Jode nodded. "It seems to be the case with this book. I wonder that Amberbirch did not know about this."

Madeline ran to the two elves who were arguing over a point of grammar. She told them about the discovery.

Amberbirch looked back calmly. "This is interesting news. I was not aware that some of the books were *Breelin*."

"How will we know which are useful this way?" Springheart demanded, his temper still hot from their argument. "We do not have time to re-read all of the books in the library."

Madeline's skin flushed with a burning itch. Her magic, missing for so long, was warning of some danger. She tried to focus it, tried to understand the warning, but, as before, she had no success. "How much of the path have you deciphered?" If they were closer to understanding the message, perhaps the hidden books were not necessary. At the thought her magic burned her skin again. Did that mean she should research the books, or that she should wait for the translation of the stones?

"We have been able to uncover the fact that there are two

messages, at least," Amberbirch said. "I am sorry that there is no clear answer."

Madeline spun on her heel and started moving back to the library. She would be no help until the message of the stones was translated into something that her sheet of paper could understand. If they needed to re-read the books, then she would start now.

Jode took her arm and stopped her headlong rush. "Wait for a moment, Madeline. Rushing around will not make this happen faster. Remember the messages from within the well. I think they are not separate versions, but one message. The gate will be closed when the one comes to decipher the clues." He drew her to a seat. "You are the one, my love. The time is now. We will figure this out."

Madeline took a breath and realized how close she had been to panic. As she released the breath, one of the children kicked her in the ribs as though to emphasize Jode's words. She laughed, rubbed her belly, and relaxed.

After a few more breaths, she calmed enough to think. "Springheart and Amberbirch, continue with the stones. Regis found three books that might be of help. We'll start by figuring out how many of those books are *Breelin*."

In the library, Jode sorted books while Regis and Madeline tried to read each of them both ways. An hour later, there were four books sitting on the *Breelin* pile.

Madeline looked at them. "If we had more translation sheets, we could be done with this today."

"I'll see what I can do," Regis said leaving the room.

"Madeline, do not wear yourself out trying to do this quickly. We have time. I feel as though we have everything we need now to solve this problem. It would be a pity for you to fall ill just when we have made this breakthrough."

By the time they had determined whether there was new information in the four books, it was full dark. Madeline found herself nodding over the last few pages of the final book. They had been unsuccessful in finding more translation sheets, so Regis and Jode had made notes while she read the pages enough to gain meaning. Despite Jode's fears, they had finished all but five pages of the *Breelin* books.

Regis was sleeping on the couch, Jode was waiting patiently for her to continue dictating notes. Madeline pinched her thigh to wake herself up enough to finish. "There's nothing more here that we didn't get from the other two," she said as she folded the book closed. "At least we have some new information." It wasn't good, but it was information.

"And we believe we have finished our discovery as well, Madeline," Springheart said as he entered the room. "Amberbirch has sent me to order you to rest. We will return to this in the morning."

Madeline knew the advice was good, but couldn't stop herself from saying, "Shouldn't we at least talk about what we've found?"

Jode took the book from her. "No, Amberbirch is right. We must confront this with fresh minds. Come to bed."

12

The next morning, breakfast on a table in the corner, jugs of caf steaming, they gathered to compare notes. More rested than she'd been in months, Madeline was optimistic, and Jode's prediction that they were almost there, had calmed her enough to let her sleep deeply. She looked at the papers laid out and thought, *yes, there's the answer.*

Her magic had nothing to say on the matter.

"I guess we should get started," she said pouring a mug of caf. "Maybe we can start with Springheart and Amberbirch telling us what they found." It was feeling a bit too much like a corporate presentation for her. With luck, they would get more out of it than she used to get out of quarterly business updates.

Springheart picked up a couple of sheets of paper. "We were fortunate in finding the meaning. Both of us agree that there are three messages in the stones and it is heartening that it matches the number within the well." He checked the paper again before continuing. "The first message is a warning about the well. When the wind blows, the time is near. When the dust rises, the enemy is preparing."

He handed Madeline the sheet. She reached for the record of

the message within the well. "It looks like this matches the first message. It's information about the well itself and how to know when it opens."

"Very good," Amberbirch said. "It took us some time to make the link." She reached for the papers Springheart was holding. "The second message we found was about the conditions. It reads 'there are three tests. The first is to decode this message. The next is to find The Stone of Lilyriver. When that is accomplished you will learn the final condition'. The final message is that the one who will seal the well will use The Stone and magic to lock the door."

Madeline looked at the two messages before handing them around. "We found only one message in the Breelin books. It was on every page of upside down writing in each book."

The message had seemed clear, but not very useful. "It was more warning about the gate, and it explains why this solution is obscure. If the wrong person tries to seal the gate, it will open wide and there will be no end to the invasion, and no rest between." If she hadn't been so tired last night, there was no way she would have been able to sleep with that knowledge. "What if I'm not the one? What if this just opens the gate?"

Jode wrapped her in his arms. "You are the one. The elven prophecy was clear on that. You are the one, do not doubt it."

Madeline took comfort from her husband's embrace, but pulled away quickly. "No one has ever told me what the prophecy said. I came here on prophecy, and at least I knew what that one said, even if I didn't understand what I was expected to do."

Regis uncurled himself from a chair by the window. "Madeline has a point. We have taken this on faith up to now, but I fear that your opinion of the clarity of the prophecy may not match ours."

Springheart looked to Amberbirch. "I would also like to know what the actual prophecy was given this new information."

Amberbirch stood and pulled her cloak close. Madeline

wasn't sure, but it seemed as though she was offended to have to explain. Springheart was right, given the fact that only one person could seal the well, it was too important to get offended at a request for some clarity.

Turning to face them, Amberbirch stood taller and took on a professorial stance. "We have a yearly ceremony where we ask for guidance. There are many things we ask for, but the most important is how to avoid the next invasion. This year, we received an answer for the first time in memory."

She paused, and Madeline had to bite her lip to stop from urging her to hurry. This information was vital, but they had to get back to figuring out this Stone of Lilyriver. Her magic flushed her skin as Amberbirch continued.

"The prophecy was surprisingly clear. Seek the woman who came between worlds, but not through the gate. She is the one. Is that sufficient to allay your suspicions?"

Yes, she was definitely offended. Madeline stepped toward Amberbirch, keeping a smile on her face, hoping to placate the elven woman. "Thank you. It wasn't suspicion. It was just a need for all of us to have the same information. One of us may find a clue that the others will miss. I am satisfied that I am The Chosen One."

Amberbirch gave a small nod and then settled back into her chair.

Regis stood to fill his plate and mug. "So, does anyone know anything about this Stone of Lilyriver? I assume we are possibly in a race with someone who wants the gate open."

Madeline's heart stopped at his words and the sudden flush of fire across her body. "I hadn't even thought about that. Do you really think someone would want to open that gate wide?" She knew that her magic was telling her something, it didn't have to be what Regis suspected. "Who would want that?"

Jode took a deep drink of caf before saying, "Someone who thought they could win against any threat that entered."

"Even the Scree would know that constant invasion would mean their death," Madeline said. "The Tryll seem content to stay in the hills. Are there other warlike creatures?"

"We do not know all the people of our world," Jode answered. "I do not know of any, but that does not mean there are none. But as you say, even the Scree would not be so foolish as to open our world to the evil that will come."

"I think we need to focus on what we can achieve and not add to our worries until we know there is a threat," Springheart said. "The Stone of Lilyriver is magical. It has not been seen for centuries."

Madeline knew it was foolish to have hoped someone would say, 'oh yes, The Stone is in the bottom drawer of that cabinet', but it did feel like a weight that had been lifted for a moment had dropped back on her shoulders. "Do we have a description? Or do we know the last location?"

"Yes, we do," Amberbirch answered. "It has the appearance of the stones that were used to create the path and well. I hope that is sufficient information."

Madeline laughed in relief that bordered on hysteria. Finally taking control again, she said, "So all we have to do is test each stone for magic?"

Amberbirch tidied the papers, not looking at Madeline as she answered, "They are all magic. I am sorry that it's not helpful, but at least we can be fairly certain that one of the stones there will be The Stone of Lilyriver."

13

Springheart watched Madeline as she organized the trip to the gate. Once more, they were going to try to decipher the message. It felt too complex to him. Even discounting the interference of the Scree, the message should have been clearer. It was strange that the knowledge had been lost, that was definitely unelven. The last battle of the gate had taken many of their bravest warriors, but the wisdom holders were always protected. He had no family to teach him his role, and so he had no role, but he knew that the first people to be evacuated in any threat were those who held the knowledge of their people.

Madeline had finished making her arrangements while he'd been lost in his thoughts. He approached her as soon as they were alone. "Madeline, are you certain it is wise to spend the night at the gate?"

She looked at him, worry stretching the fine skin of her face. "No, of course not. But we are so close. If it means we need to spend a night or two on the edge of that place, then so be it."

He drew her to a seat. "What is your magic telling you?"

She sighed and rubbed at her arms. "Nothing useful. It makes its presence known, but I can't tell if it's in warning or confirmation. I couldn't really interpret it before. The only sure thing is that something important is happening."

"Yes, I think we all know that," Springheart found himself saying. He laughed to try to lighten the mood. "What can we do to help?"

She jumped up and started pacing. "Jode will watch over us. He'll have one or two of the servants to help. Those of us with magic will have to walk the path seeking the special stone. Unless The Stone has some magical way of calling attention to itself."

"We didn't find anything in our previous visits." Springheart couldn't put aside the feeling of dread that flowed over him at the thought of the well. He told himself that it was the memory of being inside. The oddly frayed rope, the wind that seemed to suck at him, then blow him back.

"We weren't looking," Madeline responded. "If there's an answer there, we have to find it. We have precious little time. I wish Blu were here, or that Regis could find him."

He watched as she turned and paced back across the room. "You are missing your other friends too, I think. Everyone here but your husband is a stranger. You have only known us a few months."

Madeline stopped pacing. "It would be nice to have Simon to talk to. Sometimes I get tired of everything being foreign. No more than that, everything is alien to me here."

Springheart heard the loneliness in her voice. She hadn't meant to suggest that only Simon could be trusted. That thought, he knew, came from his years of isolation. "I know how it can feel when you have no family. When everything that looks familiar is not quite what you expect."

She turned and placed her hand on his arm. "I hope you'll consider us part of your family now. Springheart, if we, no when we, survive this you will always be welcome in our home."

He swallowed the lump in his throat that came with her kind words. Even Amberbirch was only polite to him. And that was because he might be of service in sealing the gate. He would be of service even if that meant he had to become a sacrifice. That's what his intuition was telling him. That there would be a need for a sacrifice, and an important one. "I would be honored."

She moved away again. He could sense her tension vibrating through the air. Suddenly she turned to face him. "I need to ask you to do something. You might not want to, but I know you can do this thing." Her face had gone white, and Springheart knew her thoughts had been aligned with his.

"I will die to make this a success," he said.

She sat beside him. "You know, don't you? This ceremony is going to require a sacrifice. There's no way it would have to wait for The Chosen One if there wasn't a specific need."

Yes, he thought. "An elf without a family is rare and specific. If needed, I will willingly sacrifice my life."

She shook her head. "No, I don't think it will be you. I think it's me. I'm from another world but didn't come through the gate."

He sat back at her words. "I did not think of that. It is not certain that you have been chosen as the sacrifice."

"I'm going to ask you to do something hard, Springheart. If it turns out that I must go into the well, I need you to stop Jode following me. I want him to live. I need to know he'll be safe until people can help him heal." She sobbed on the last words then tears flooded her cheeks.

Springheart wasn't sure what to do, but as she leaned into him, he placed his arm around her and allowed her to empty her heart. "I will make sure he is safe. I promise." He felt her struggle to regain control.

"Thank you," she managed to say through her sniffles.

Standing, Springheart retrieved a napkin from the breakfast table and handed it to her. "Madeline, remember, we do not know what the sacrifice will be. Do not be too eager to die for this."

She wiped her eyes and nose with the napkin and managed a watery smile. "Believe me, I have no desire to die. I will if needed, but I want there to be a different answer. I want to grow old with Jode and my children. But I'm losing confidence that we can have both."

He saw her body flush as she said the words. "Is that your magic?"

She rubbed at her arms. "Yes. Apparently, it's trying to tell me something, but I don't speak its language."

He laughed. "If anything about this prophecy is predictable, it is that there will always be more than one answer. Perhaps we will be faced with a choice of sacrifices and consequences."

Madeline looked at him, eyes wide. She rubbed harder at her skin. "That may be truer than you think."

"Then we will look forward to solving this problem and not to the argument over who will be the sacrifice." He turned his head to the door. "I hear Jode calling. The preparations are complete."

MADELINE HELPED to unpack the wagon when they arrived, her mind drifting to the edge of the stone spiral while the others set up the camp. As she listened to the bustle behind her, Madeline looked over the passage to the gate. Now that they were back in their original places, it was clear that the pattern they'd seen was not intended by the makers. Even without sending her magical senses into the stones, she could feel the rightness of the setting. From this angle, she could see how smooth the spiral was laid, almost as if the individual pavers were only etched out of one huge stone disk.

There was nothing to indicate that The Stone of Lilyriver was different from the others. Madeline realized that she had been unconsciously hoping that it would glow or rise up when she got near. "Let's hope it's not one of the ones inside the well," she muttered.

"What was that?" Regis asked as he joined her.

"Nothing," Madeline answered, hoping to keep her fears from gaining life. "Do you think there's any way we can apply logic? There must be a reason for the Stone's location."

He chuckled and said, "It was placed by elves. Their reason may seem completely random to anyone else."

Before she could respond, Amberbirch and Springheart joined them. "If we try to understand why The Stone might be in its place, we might spend years doing nothing else," Amberbirch said. "Jode has agreed to stand back while we walk the path. I have assured him that we will not approach the edge of the well unless we are tethered."

Madeline looked over her shoulder at her husband. He stood tall, arms crossed, and a scowl on his face. "Thank you for that. I don't think we could be effective if we were tied together. And we would be too much weight for him to hold if something happened."

"How close can we get?" Regis asked. "If we have to stop before we get to the center, we may miss The Stone."

Springheart stepped onto the first paver. "We left that unclear. If we walk in a line and Madeline is at the end, then I suggest we can get two or three spirals in before Jode will race to the rescue."

Madeline pictured Jode running across the stones to haul her back to camp. "Yes, if we cross the line he has imagined to be safety, he won't wait for something to happen. We'll have to figure out something else to do tonight if The Stone isn't apparent." She stepped forward. "Springheart, come back. I think if I'm The Chosen, I should try it alone first." She hoped they would be able to keep Jode from overreacting.

She waved away the objections and waited for Springheart to stand behind her with the others. When they were arranged, she lowered herself to sit cross-legged on the grass. At this angle, she could still see across the stones to the well, and it was easier to pick out the edges of the individual pavers. "I'm going to try to find it with my magic. Don't break my concentration unless I stop breathing, or keel over."

Madeline made them all agree before continuing. "All of the stones are magic, right? The Lilyriver one should be different magic which means I can pick it out."

Amberbirch answered, "Yes, my understanding of the legend is that when The Stone is discovered, there is no doubt as to its genuineness."

Madeline felt relieved at the thought they wouldn't have to pick out The Stone of Lilyriver from decoys. "The magic of all of the stones is to preserve them from erosion. What will happen when we pull out one of them?"

"I do not have that knowledge," Amberbirch admitted. "If you look at them with your power, you should be able to see the answer. But even if the spell collapses, the stones will only weather naturally, they will not fall to dust."

"Okay. I'll be back," Madeline said. No one recognized the quote and she missed Simon all the more.

Settling into the pose, Madeline placed her hand on her abdomen. It felt comforting to feel the bulge of her children. "I need you to be quiet for a little while," she murmured. There was no response.

Madeline smiled and let her magic flow across the stones. As it touched, her sight changed from the clear light of the afternoon to a dimmer, cooler glow. The stones glowed a warm orange as her power passed. Within seconds the entire stone path glowed the same color. The only difference was the center. The well glowed black. It wasn't just deep and dark; it emanated a sense of blackness that Madeline had never encountered before. She kept her attention away from the darkness and looked for details in the spell that her power had exposed.

She concentrated and found herself sinking into the magic. In her mind, she stood on the stones in a position about halfway between the grass and the well. Her image bent and Madeline was able to see that the spell was a web. It connected each stone of the path. When it reached those stones circling the well, the color faded to a more yellow tone. She realized there were at least two layers of spell. The yellow one protected all the stones, and another did something else. She couldn't penetrate the yellow layer to see what lay underneath.

Madeline started to pull herself out of the trance so that she could ask for advice. The dim light was brightening, the feeling of warmth from the sun entering her consciousness, when Madeline felt the world tilt. As her consciousness receded, the yellow blanket of the spell lifted and wrapped itself around her.

14

She woke looking up at the concerned faces of her friends. Her head was in Jode's lap, and he was stroking her forehead. "Welcome back," he said, relief coloring his words. "Please do not do that again."

Madeline struggled to get up. She wanted to stay in Jode's arms, but she knew there was still work to do.

She told them what had happened. "I think it was the children," she finished.

Amberbirch knelt beside her. "We did not see anything other than you settling into the trance. You were only there for seconds when your body collapsed onto the grass."

Madeline pushed herself up to stand. "The red glow is still there; can you see it?" She turned to the others. If she didn't need a trance to see it, surely they could. When no one spoke, she asked, "You can't see it, can you?"

Regis shook his head. "It still looks the same to me. Do you see anything that indicates The Stone of Lilyriver?"

She shook her head. It looked like she was the only one who would be of help. She rubbed her bulging belly and felt the squirm of movement that told her the babies were playing. There had to be a way to show the others. "Give me your hand, Spring-heart." When they clasped hands, she continued, "I'm going into a trance, and I'll try to bring you with me. If it works, you need to tell me what you see."

Springheart nodded and gestured for the others to stand ready to catch them if they collapsed.

Madeline closed her eyes and pictured the circle as she'd last seen it. When the vision was clear she squeezed Springheart's hand and thought his name. He was standing beside her as soon as she finished the word. He squeezed back and she looked at him.

He turned toward the circle, nodded, and then returned his gaze to her. Madeline saw surprise lift his expression as he dropped his eyes to her belly. She followed his gaze and jerked her hand from his. Then everything went dark.

"I asked you not to do that again," Jode's voice drew her back to consciousness.

She jerked upright and looked at the mound of her pregnancy. "They have magic. It was there with us." She looked up at Spring-heart. "You saw it."

He nodded. "Two ribbons of power led from your womb across the spiral of stones. I saw the red glow and, I think the children were seeking something. I hope it was the same thing as we are."

"We have to go back. I know we'll find it," she struggled to rise again, but Jode held her tight.

"Wait," he said. "We are not certain that they are seeking. What if the well is drawing them, drawing all of you?" His worry tightened his arms around her.

Madeline patted his arm, knowing that he must be afraid. Sad that he had no magic so he couldn't experience what they did, she said, "I know it is not. Please, trust us. We only have a few hours of daylight. If the wind and dust stay away, we may be able to find The Stone and get back to the library tonight."

He kissed the top of her head and released her. "You will all be tied together, and I will drag you back if something happens. I do not care if the stones rub your skin raw. If something happens to you, I will make sure you are safe."

Tears pressed on Madeline's eyes. She wished that he didn't have to go through this alone. If Simon were here, they would be able to support each other through the time when everyone was dealing in magical searches. "I think with the children helping, we can confine the search party to me and one other. I think Regis will be my best companion. Between us we will have the most magic. And he has had contact with the children, which means he might be able to help."

No one argued. Madeline didn't know whether she felt relief or disappointment. She knew it didn't matter. They would be done with this before night. Her magic didn't have any predictions, but she knew.

"I don't know what will happen," she said as she took Regis' hand. "When we get into the trance, you'll see that the stones are bathed in red. It's a spell, but I don't know what it is for."

"Should we try to find the purpose?" He stood still while Jode tied a rope around his waist.

Madeline tested the knots on her own tether before answering. She had no plan, just a hope that The Stone would be identifiable. "Yes. Perhaps finding the reason for the spell will be the key." She placed her hand on her bump. "Do you hear me, kids? Don't go off on your own."

Regis raised an eyebrow. "Do you think that will work?"

She laughed. "I can only hope, but I feel like our plan will depend on what these little brats will want us to do."

They stepped onto the stone. Madeline entered her trance. Her eyes flew open as she heard Regis gasp. The stones were no longer just covered in red as though stained, they glowed and vibrated. "That's new," she said. Her words were calm, but her heart was beating its way out of her chest. "Do you see anything helpful?" She wanted his opinion without her guidance. If her own wishes were affecting the spell, she wouldn't know otherwise.

He pointed as he spoke. "The spell ends before the well, but I see no stone otherwise that stands out."

"Can you tell what the spell is?" Madeline waited patiently as Regis bent to touch the power beneath their feet.

"It seems to be concealment," he said, rising. "It seems that our designers did everything they could to make this puzzle close to impossible for the wrong person to find the Stone."

Madeline looked out over the circle. "Let's hope it's not the same for us. I think we should start moving. Between the vibration of the stones and the impending wind, I'm having to force myself not to run."

She stepped forward, but Regis pulled her back. "The stones vibrate?"

"Yes, can't you feel it? It's not unpleasant, but it is making me want to move." The vibration was low and gentle, almost massaging her legs.

"I feel nothing," Regis said, shrugging.

Madeline pulled him a step forward, the vibration disappeared.

Regis squeezed her hand. "Wait, now I feel it. It is not unpleasant."

Her skin flushed. "That's the key. Let's keep going."

The next step changed the reaction again. Neither Regis nor Madeline felt vibration, but the babies suddenly became active, kicking at her ribs. "That doesn't feel like they are happy," she said, rubbing her side after a particularly hard kick. They moved to the next step, Regis moaned and pulled her along. "That is better. What do you feel?"

Madeline waited for any reaction from inside. "I feel the good vibration, and the babies seem to feel nothing. You?"

"The pleasant vibration. So, have we learned enough? I would like to think we can move quickly. You do not want to experience the unpleasant one for more than a second or two. In your condition, it is likely to bring on your sickness again."

"I think it's a matter of crossing the stones until we all feel one reaction. Let's hope it's the pleasant one." Madeline waited for her skin to flush, but nothing happened. "Let's move quickly. If I'm wrong, then we will have time to try something else before the light is gone."

Regis smiled. "And if you are right, we will be one step closer to the solution."

"If you feel the right reaction, speak. Otherwise we keep moving forward. I'll speak for the babies." Madeline hoped that their reaction would be as fast as hers.

Moving rapidly, they covered more than half of the stones before feeling in tune. "I guess that's it," Madeline said as her vision suddenly filled with golden light, and she felt four separate vibrations in her heart.

She dropped her smallest knife on the stone and released them from the spell.

They packed up the camp while Jode and one of the strongest servants used a metal bar to lift The Stone of Lilyriver from the circle. It came up more easily than expected. Since the discovery, it was as though the neighboring pavers had shrunk back enough to allow them to get leverage.

By the time they were back in the library, The Stone safely inside and brushed clean of most of the dirt that coated the underside, it was late. Both Madeline and Regis were falling asleep. The magic had drained their energy. Springheart and Amberbirch offered to clean The Stone and inspect it for the morning. Madeline allowed Jode to tuck her in and fell into a deep sleep.

15

The next morning, she awoke feeling hope for a change. Today could be the end of the quest. With The Stone in their hands, she was sure the answer was within their grasp. And there was no sign that anyone else was seeking it. The fear that someone would open the gate had slipped away during her sleep. Blu would be here soon, and he would arrive in time for the celebration, rather than come to the rescue.

She went searching for everyone and found them in the library by following the sound of raised voices. This was the first time she'd heard them argue loudly. Past disagreements had been discussed quietly and reasoned out as much as possible. This argument was heated, but she couldn't make out the subject.

As she approached, Regis stormed out of the room. On encountering Madeline, he said, "I am sorry, Madeline, I must take some time to cool down."

She tried to stop him so she could ask what had happened, but he rushed past toward the kitchens. As she turned, Springheart hurried past without a word. She watched him go through the front door before rushing into the room. "What is going on?"

Jode stopped in mid-sentence and turned to her. "It's about time you woke up," he snapped at her.

Her normally kind and patient husband was blazing anger. "Answer me," she snapped back, telling herself she would only be able to calm him by starting on his level. She ignored the stab of pleasure she felt at being able to say what she really meant, rather than couching her request in flowery language.

Amberbirch sneered. "There is some disagreement about our next action. The others wrongly believe that The Stone is sending us to the forest, or the river, to find the answer. I have made the correct interpretation. We must go to the mountains."

"That is ridiculous, woman," Jode shouted. "The mountains are far too long a journey for us to undertake in time."

Amberbirch started to answer, but Madeline shouted her down. "Stop it now! This is not helping. I don't know why everyone has made such decisions without me. I am The Chosen One. I will know what is to be done!" She waited for them to agree, but they just glared at her.

The room felt like an oven, the fury heating it to an unbearable level. Her next words were stolen by the gasp of pain as she received kicks in her ribs and kidneys. The red rage that had overcome her faded slightly with the pain.

"Please, stop this." Springheart's words were calm and quiet, more like his usual self. "Come out of the room."

Madeline spun to face him. "Who are you to tell me what to do?"

He held up his hand to quiet their reactions. "It is The Stone. Come from the room, and you will see the difference."

Regis appeared behind the elf. "He is right. Come out and we can all discuss what we have found."

The words just spurred her determination to make them understand her position in this group. She stamped toward them, ignoring Jode and Amberbirch. "I will not rely on your interpretation." As she neared Springheart, his hand darted out to grab her arm and drag her through the opening.

"Regis, take her farther away until the effect is gone."

Madeline found herself passed to Regis who started walking away, forcing her to match his pace. "Stop it. You have no right…" As she moved away from the room the rage faded and embarrassment flooded her. "Oh shit! How are we going to figure out the next step?"

Regis stopped and faced her. "Let's start by bringing the other two into a place of sanity."

Madeline followed him back to the room. Jode was threatening to run his sword through Springheart for touching his wife, and Amberbirch was urging him on. "Why are they so bad?"

Regis pushed her forward. "They were there when we arrived. I don't know how long they have been under the influence. It seems that the longer you have been there, the more time you need to calm down. Your mood changed far faster than mine. Talk to him."

Madeline shook her head. "Neither of them is listening. If we rush them and drag them out, we'll be better off. Look, Amberbirch is almost within arm's reach." She told Springheart to grab the elven woman while Regis took his other hand and made sure he didn't enter the room.

When Amberbirch was in the hall, Springheart took her away. The woman retained the anger the entire time she was in earshot. Madeline turned her attention back to Jode. "I don't know if we can do that to him. I think he means to use his weapon."

Regis agreed. "He will not come close enough anyway. Look."

Madeline saw that Jode was backing away. The Stone sat on its side in the center of the room. Madeline watched the color fade from her husband's face. He looked at her with horror. "What happened to us?"

She took a step forward and Regis halted her. "If you go in, it will start again. One person has no one to fight with."

Stepping back again, Madeline called Jode to join them in the hall. He didn't argue as he stepped out of the room. They joined Amberbirch and Springheart in the kitchen.

"The problem seems to be that I'm the one who will find the solution," Madeline said as they gathered around a table. "But I don't read Elvish."

Jode nodded. "The writing we found under The Stone was in old Elvish. Amberbirch translated almost half of it before we started arguing." He flushed at the memory. "I am truly sorry for my behavior."

Amberbirch waved away his apology. "We were under the influence of a spell. I do not hold you accountable." She looked at Regis and Springheart. "I hope we will all dismiss the words that were exchanged."

As they blushed and nodded, Madeline wondered exactly how bad the fight had been. "The only thing we need to remember is that no more than one person can be in the room at a time. So, will my translation sheet work for this?" She knew the answer but hoped there was a solution that allowed her to read the source, rather than someone's translation.

"No, it was created for you to use it on books," Springheart said. "It may not recognize the words carved in the stone."

"I have thought of this as my mind returned to sanity," Amberbirch said. "I can go in and create a translation. Then Springheart can go in and create a separate translation. Then you can read them. You will not need to go into the room."

Madeline frowned. Was there a reason Amberbirch wanted to keep her from the room? "I would prefer to see The Stone myself."

"I worry that the children will have an effect on you in the room," Amberbirch said calmly. "It may be that the spell will see them as separate people. Do you wish to risk yourself in a fight with them? When your reason is taken away."

She had a point, but Madeline felt suspicion claw at her. There was no reason for it, but she felt the sensation growing.

Before she could speak, Jode said, "And how do we know that your translation will be true? Two elves can be in collusion, and we would have no way of knowing."

Madeline rose. "Wait, we are arguing again. We need to get farther away." She marched toward the front door. "That stone is still affecting us." The suspicion fell away a few steps out of the building. "This is far enough for now. How does everyone feel?"

"I do not know how long it will last," Regis said, "but I am feeling as though we are a team again."

Madeline would have preferred to move farther, but they needed a plan. When it was worked out, they would separate and she would go alone into the library. If the children were seen as separate by the spell. They could try the other approach.

"If I had your translation sheet, perhaps I could change the spell to read this version of Elvish," Amberbirch said, turning back to the library. "I can go back and get it."

Madeline held her back. "No. Regis can go. If the spell keeps extending so that the servants are affected I would rather you were here to calm them."

Regis bowed low. "I am pleased to be the sacrifice for this. Where is your sheet?"

Madeline laughed at his clowning and told him where she'd last used the translation sheet. "While he's gone, can you tell me how far you got?"

Amberbirch looked at the others and they nodded for her to speak. "We only got through half of the translation. Like everything, there is more than one answer. We did not argue that there was no journey, just about the destination."

Madeline nodded her understanding. "Is there a reason stated for the journey?"

Springheart answered, "I think it is because the final answer will be at the place. Unfortunately, we cannot visit more than one of the possibilities before we must seal the gate."

Madeline sighed. "Well let's hope that we can figure out which of these is the right one. At least we know that there's no one else going after it. The Stone hasn't been disturbed since it was set."

"Not that you noticed," Jode reminded her. "You only went back to the time when the Scree moved some of them. It is possible that The Stone was discovered before that."

Madeline winced at the kick she received from one of the twins. She tried not to think of it as a response to Jode's words. Kids kicked for no reason other than movement. "Let's work on the assumption we are the only ones."

Regis returned with the sheet.

"The servants will go to the village and only return when we call them. We are now in charge of our own food," Amberbirch said before taking the page and placing her right hand on it while humming. The sheet flickered as though it was backlit, changing from the color of pale velum to a bone white then back to velum. "It is ready. Will you go now?"

Madeline couldn't see any reason to delay. The longer they stayed here, the more likely they would feel the effect of the spell and start fighting again. "You should wait at the lake to be safe from its influence. I wonder how we managed to transport The Stone without the spell affecting us."

"The words were covered in dirt while we transported it," Springheart answered. "Perhaps if you covered them again, it will stop the effect."

"I'll try," Madeline said as she headed toward the library.

She mused while she made her way along the path to the library. Was there a way for her to test the veracity of the translation? There were no books in the library that she hadn't been able to read. Then it came to her. The words from the other stones. The ones she had to get as a translation from Springheart and Amberbirch.

She searched through the papers scattered on the sideboard to find the transcription of the words on the stones. Placing the translation sheet on top, she read the words, 'The Stone of Lilyriver is the twentieth stone from the center. Remove the two layers of spells, and you shall be able to remove the one you need.'

She stared at the words. They couldn't have missed such a clear message. Had they colluded to misdirect the answer? As soon as the thought was complete, she dismissed it. There was no benefit for either of the elves to undermine their quest. Their people were the first line of defense.

"This is just proof that I am The Chosen. The message was only there for me to read," she muttered. Turning to look at the stone, she saw that it was larger than the sheet of magical paper. Would it make a difference?

Madeline knelt beside The Stone and placed the translation sheet up to the top. 'The Chosen will know the right path.' Madeline smiled in relief and kept reading. 'A journey will be required to find the last item. To the valley of the Oak Tree. It will give The Chosen One the words to speak and the time to act.'

Madeline ran from the room and gathered a handful of moss and dirt from under a nearby tree. Returning, she packed the side of The Stone with enough of the dirt to obscure the words. A feeling of lightness flowed through her as she covered the Stone. They would send to the village and have the servants return it to its place in the spiral.

She made her way back to the lake to gather the others. Springheart went to the village to call the servants back to the library and everyone else gathered in the kitchen to wait.

Madeline told them what she had found. "It seems that I am the only one who can see the clues clearly. There was no other interpretation," she said, leaving out the message directing her to The Stone in the first place. "How long will it take us to get to the valley of the Oak Tree?"

Amberbirch stared at the message that Madeline had written

out on the scrap of paper. "We should have spent all this time teaching you to read the ancient language," she muttered. "So much time wasted."

Madeline sat beside her. "Don't think about what we could have done. We have the solution and the there is still time."

Amberbirch shook her head as she touched the words. Madeline realized that woman needed time to get over what she thought of as her personal failure. She looked at Jode to send him away and saw him nod before she could speak. He slipped out taking Regis with him.

Madeline turned back to Amberbirch. She didn't know what to say about the past, but she knew that it always helped her if she focused on the next step when things were going wrong. To do everything she could to plow through to the next success.

"We need to get going to the Valley of the Oak Tree," she said gently. "Let's get ready for that. You can teach me the ancient tongue while we travel."

Amberbirch looked up. "Yes," she said, clarity coming to her eyes. "It is only two days' travel. What happens when we arrive? Do you know how we will find the words?"

Madeline hated to break the new confidence that Amberbirch was showing, but knew that the truth would be better in the end. "No, but I assume it will be something I can see. Having come this far, it has to be easy, even if it is only easy for me."

Handing the paper back to her, Amberbirch rose and said, "When the servants return, we can prepare. I would have us leave early tomorrow to avoid camping an extra night. If we leave just after dawn, it will make little difference to the time we arrive in the valley. And we will know that The Stone has been returned."

Madeline was surprised at the speed that the elven woman had recovered, but she willingly accepted it, not wanting to look for trouble. "Good. I'll let the others know."

Amberbirch looked at Madeline with puzzlement on her face. "I am curious as to why you allow Regis so much freedom."

"He has been very helpful. I know he came to us with a terrible history, but he has shown himself willing to change." Madeline had come to think of Regis as a friend. Even Jode seemed to have forgiven his past acts.

"I heard that he was responsible for attacks on a child, a baby. It is not something I would have forgiven, even if the child were not related to him."

"Yes, I thought that I would never be able to understand, let alone forgive. But he was angry and hurt. Nothing happened to Tadric, and he will become a co-regent. If Tadric's mother can forgive him, I can." Madeline was not sure that Arabela would forgive Regis, at least not right away. She would rely on the oaths and that would give her time to know the real Regis.

The elven woman nodded. "Humans are different from elves. To us, family is everything. No one would consider attacking their own."

Madeline's patience was running out. Amberbirch was right about humans being different. Springheart was lost without his family. The elves treated him politely, but no one was close to him. He'd have no home here ever. "Humans are different. We recognize that everyone needs family, and we can create family from strangers."

Amberbirch looked down at the paper that was sitting on the table. "Perhaps this is because you are so short lived. When you live for centuries, you learn that people do not change. Eventually everyone returns to their true self."

"Yes, we know that too. But we are willing to accept that someone's worst behavior is not their true self." This discussion was not going anywhere, and it was not going to change her mind. Regis would be with them. "I think we all need a rest. The effect of the spell has worn us down."

Madeline saw that Amberbirch was about to say something, then her face relaxed. "You are right. It may be exhaustion, but I caution you not to place your trust so easily. Elven or human, people are complicated. It is possible to seem like you are helping when you have a separate agenda."

Amberbirch left before Madeline could answer her comment. It left her feeling weary, not just from the work she'd done, nor from her pregnancy, but in her heart. As much as she wanted to deny Amberbirch, her words were true. No matter how hard people tried, they always acted true to their understanding of the world. They only changed because their understanding of the world changed. Like hers had.

Needing to do something positive, something that was either right or wrong, and no shades of maybe, she went back to the room where The Stone of Lilyriver lurked on its frame. Glaring at it, Madeline picked up the sketch Regis had made of the spiral. The words were in a language she couldn't read, and the stones were not in the right order, but it should work as a test. She placed the translation sheet on top. She shouldn't see a message, the instructions to The Stone should not be there because of the stones being moved. Something had been nagging at her since the vision of the Scree. Why had he chosen those stones? To make it work, he would have to pick the stones and drop chalk. It might have been random, but that seemed too easy.

She looked at the page and her fears were made real. There was a new message, one she would keep to herself.

The Chosen will be betrayed. The sacrifice will determine the outcome.

The Scree was delivering a warning, not sabotaging the future.

16

They headed out early in the morning. Madeline hadn't slept well, wondering all night who would be the one to betray her. The ride in the wagon wasn't helping, the movement kept her feeling nauseated. Not enough to make her sick, but enough to make her uneasy. She knew that there were only two people she fully trusted, Jode and herself. There were too many reasons that the others might not be loyal. Almost as many reasons that they should be trusted.

Up to now, she hadn't thought about any of this. She'd trusted everyone. Even Regis. Even after all he'd done to Tadric, she'd believed that he was helping.

And Springheart. She hadn't doubted anything he'd told her.

"Madeline, you are very quiet," Jode said. "Is there something I can do to cheer you up?"

Unless he had some way of sorting out who will betray them, no. "I'm sorry. I guess the pregnancy is getting to that stage." It made her angry that she felt the need to lie. Was this how it started?

"This will be an easy ride. Rest when we stop." He reached out and caressed her cheek. "I hope this will be the last thing you need to find. I think you need to become a pampered wife who has no worries on her mind. One who does not have to save her friends, or the world."

Madeline leaned into his caress, feeling the love flow between them. "It would be nice to spend a little time getting fat and motherly."

"That's the attitude. I'd like a fat wife." He laughed at her grimace and moved his horse away.

Her mood lightened as she watched him move along the line of riders. There were three elven guards along with the five of them. The assurances that they were safe were severely undercut by the addition of the guards.

Madeline snapped the reins and urged the wagon horses forward. Trying not to go on the search for betrayal clues, she talked to Amberbirch. "What are the guards for again?"

The elven woman sat her horse as though she were born to it. She turned to Madeline and said, "Probably nothing, but I feel better knowing that they are there. If we need someone to do manual labor at the end of this journey, we will find them helpful."

Madeline couldn't fault the reasoning, so she changed tactics. "This may be the end of our quest. I'm hoping that we will be able to perform the ceremony in the next day or so."

"Let us hope that it is so simple." Amberbirch smiled, but Madeline felt the sarcasm salting her tone.

Laughing, Madeline said, "It would be nice for a change."

"Down!" The shout came from the lead elf.

Madeline slid out off the wagon bench and ran to hide behind the trunk of a large tree. Amberbirch joined her. Peeking around the trunk, Madeline saw shadows flitting from tree to tree ahead of their party. Jode, Regis, Springheart, and the three elves were trying to engage the shadows, but it looked like they were not going to be successful.

Amberbirch shifted beside Madeline. "Do you have weapons?"

Touching the hilts of her knives, Madeline nodded. "What are those things?"

"There are some creatures who live in these hills. They are usually not willing to engage such a large party," Amberbirch answered.

Madeline pulled her knives and kept her reaction to herself. If there were creatures between them and the Valley of the Oak Trees, then she should have known. "What kind of creatures?"

Amberbirch didn't have time to answer. "Look," she said pointing ahead.

Madeline saw the three elf guards fighting with the shadows. Their blades seemed to slice through smoke, doing no damage to the attackers. As she watched, Jode and Springheart ran to help, and Regis ran back toward her and Amberbirch.

"Stay low ladies," he said as he crouched beside them. "These damn people are fast. They are bandits, and we will be fine if there are no more of them."

Madeline weighed her knives, and placed all but the longest one back in their sheaths. The attackers were moving too quickly for throwing knives to be effective. "Elven bandits? Or something else?"

Amberbirch flushed. "Elven. Those without family sometimes choose the wrong path. That is why family is so important."

Regis moved to stand beside Madeline who had risen. "Springheart is honorable. He is fighting as hard and anyone to keep us safe."

Madeline spared a second to look back at Amberbirch. The woman's expression was cold. Before she could say anything else that hinted at Springheart's lack of loyalty, Madeline responded, "It must be difficult when family is so important to be so harshly excluded if you have none. The elves might be better served by bringing orphans into the fold rather than pushing them to the edges." Despite not knowing who she could trust, Madeline could not bear the cruelty elves showed to their own people.

Regis stepped forward as one of the shadows moved toward them through the trees. "Do you have any weapons, Amberbirch?"

"None." The word was snapped out.

"Then stay behind us," Madeline instructed as she stepped beside Regis.

Now that they were close, Madeline could see that the shadow was a female elf. She looked to be very young, perhaps not even in her teens. She was thin, her cheekbones prominent, her eyes violet and huge, white blond hair knotted into a braid that swung as she dodged. Then the child moved, and Madeline wondered at what she'd seen.

The fight was fast, faster than Madeline had practiced, but she focused only on stopping the elf from making contact with her blade. She felt Regis beside her, matching the pace of her movements. The elf tried to move around them to get to Amberbirch, but was not able to break through their line, nor was she fast enough to move around them.

Suddenly Regis gasped and faltered. Madeline kept slashing at the elf who seemed to gain a new strength. Prepared for Regis to fall back, hoping that Amberbirch would pull him away, and praying that the others would come to her aid, Madeline almost speared him as he pitched forward and fell on the attacker.

The two lay on the ground unmoving. Madeline rushed to feel for a pulse in Regis' neck. It was there, but faint. She checked the elf; the child was unconscious. "Amberbirch, help me," Madeline called as she turned Regis over. The elven sword was lodged in his side.

Amberbirch crawled to them. "You need to remove the sword before I can heal him," she said, coldly efficient.

Madeline took the hilt in her hands and called on all of her strength and anger to pull it cleanly out. She knew that it could make things worse if she didn't remove the weapon in the same path it entered.

Blood gushed out of Regis when the sword was removed. Madeline heard running footsteps and stood with the sword out to meet the attack. Jode skidded to a halt with the other defenders behind.

He looked at Regis on the ground. "We have stopped the attack. What happened? Are you hurt?" He reached for the sword, but Madeline dropped it to the ground before throwing herself into his arms.

"Regis... he fell on her blade." Madeline tried not to succumb to the tears that threatened to blind her. *Damn hormones.*

Jode held her close and she heard him direct the others to bind the unconscious elf, then ask Amberbirch for a report. Madeline pulled away to hear the news.

"He will be fine, but it will take time for him to regain his strength."

Relief washed over her, taking away the suspicion she'd felt about him. His act had been to save and protect, there was no doubt in her mind that he was loyal. "Should we send him back to the library? We can spare one of the guards."

"Absolutely not." Regis's voice was weak but steady. "I have spent the last few months in boring research. I will not be sent away just as we are getting to the interesting parts."

Madeline decided that they would make camp where they were. She worked with Springheart to build a strong dome of protection around them. They made Regis rest, leaving Amberbirch to ensure he would regain his strength.

The elven girl was tied to a tree while they set up. Madeline noticed that when she regained consciousness, the girl kept her eyes closed. It was apparent in the way her body changed from completely relaxed to tense and wary, that she was aware of her surroundings.

"What are we going to do with her?" Madeline asked Jode. "She's a child, but she would have killed Regis."

"We cannot leave her tied there. If her friends do not free her, she will die before we return. If her friends do come back, they will know where we have gone."

Madeline sighed; this was a no win situation. "I'll talk to her. Let's see if we can take her with us. Even if she's tied up the whole way, she might be better off in our party. She doesn't look like she's eaten enough for weeks."

The guards had made a stew from their supplies. The aroma was making Madeline's stomach growl. She didn't want to think about what this child felt. Taking a bowl and spoon from the guard, Madeline approached the elf. "I know you are awake. You must be hungry," she said as she lowered herself to the ground next to the tree. The pregnancy was starting to affect her agility, and she almost spilled the stew as she struggled with her balance.

The girl was staring at Madeline, so she held the bowl up to catch her eye. "Are you hungry?" She dipped the spoon and held out a portion.

The girl eyed it suspiciously. "If you want to kill me, fight. Poison is the coward's way."

Madeline laughed and ate the spoonful. "See, it is fine to eat."

Watching Madeline chew and swallow the food, the child licked her lips. "I can feed myself."

"No. Until we know you can be trusted, I'll feed you." Madeline took another spoonful and offered it.

The girl opened her mouth, eyes still wary, but obviously too hungry to let her suspicion rule. As she chewed, she closed her eyes, a smile tugging at the corner of her lips.

"It's good, isn't it?" Madeline asked. "Will you tell me your name?"

"Is that the price of this food?"

Madeline shook her head and offered another spoonful. "I was hoping not to think of you only as the child who attacked my friend. My name is Madeline."

"What happened to the others? The ones I came with?" The child asked after swallowing. "Did you kill them all?"

97

Madeline didn't know how many bandits had been killed or injured, but she knew some had escaped. "No, some left. Why did you attack?"

"We were hungry," she said looking at the bowl in Madeline's hand. "It is hard to live here. There are few animals, and they are quick."

Madeline continued to feed her while they talked. "I am sorry that you have to live out here. Could you have gone somewhere? In The City, perhaps you could have found employment."

The girl glared at her. "We are elves. This is where we live."

Madeline didn't ask any other questions until the stew was gone. She helped the girl sip from a mug of water. "We need to decide what to do with you."

"You mean how you are going to kill me?"

"That would be a waste of stew," Madeline said. "We'll find a way to bring you with us. When we have completed our task, we'll figure out what's next."

"Why are you being so nice to me?" The puzzlement on the girl's face was echoed in her voice. She really had expected to be killed.

Madeline pushed herself up from the ground. "My friend is going to be okay, and I think you had no choice."

"My name is Willowvine."

Madeline smiled. "Thank you." She thought it would be better to let Willowvine think over her options. And one mouthful of the stew had only exacerbated her hunger. Joining the others around the small fire, she served herself from the pot.

Amberbirch joined her. "Regis is recovering his strength. He will be fit to ride tomorrow."

"Will we still be able to get to our destination in a day?" Madeline asked.

Amberbirch glanced at their prisoner. "If she does not slow us down. We will arrive a few hours before sunset. Still time to do some searching."

Madeline hoped that would be enough. She longed for the security of the library. "Why would these elves stay here? Even without families, there must be opportunity for them outside in the wider world."

Springheart sat beside her. "For an elf, this land is like a mother. I only leave because I have business outside in the world. But I am doing elven business. If I had to rely on work from the Mariai, or humans, I would not last long."

"So, living in the wild in your own land is better than that life." Madeline despaired of understanding elves. "We'll have to find a way to constrain her other than the ropes."

"There is a spell," Amberbirch said.

"No." Springheart's voice was quiet but carried a depth that Madeline had never heard before. "You cannot subject her to that. An oath will do."

Amberbirch's eyes narrowed, and she seemed on the verge of arguing.

"What spell?" Madeline asked. "What oath?"

Amberbirch pointed to Springheart who said, "The spell will subjugate the child's will. An oath will keep her from attacking, or running away, while we need her."

"Okay, can you get her to take the oath?" Madeline stretched out the kinks in her back.

"If that is what you prefer," Amberbirch said, pulling her cloak around her as if needing armor. "She trusts you, or as much as she can trust anyone. I am sure you will have the most success."

"I would prefer if she was willing to join us without coercion," Madeline said. "Why do you think we need the added incentive of the spell?"

The woman turned to look at Willowvine. Madeline's gaze followed hers to see that the child was testing the knots binding her to the tree. It was no different from what any of them would do in the same circumstances, but Amberbirch seemed to be reading more than a normal response into her actions.

After a moment, Amberbirch said, "She is without family. I cannot say how she will react. No one has taught her the right way to live."

Madeline glanced at Springheart. The words applied to him as well, but he didn't seem offended, just tired. He smiled back and said, "It is how we think, Madeline."

It didn't matter to Madeline. She would not use magic when an oath would do. If Willowvine was unwilling, they would leave a guard with her. "The oath is better, Amberbirch. I would rather she be given a choice."

The elven woman glanced at Willowvine again before answering, "It is your decision, Chosen One." She straightened and moved to her bedroll.

Madeline watched Amberbirch as she settled in. It was only early afternoon, but the woman was obviously going to ignore them for the rest of the day.

Springheart tapped her on the arm. "I can help you with the oath, Madeline. If we do it now, she can be freed. I hate to see her so tied up."

Madeline took her attention from Amberbirch. "I'll let Regis know. I'd hate for him to be surprised when she's walking free."

When she checked on him, Regis dismissed her concern. "She's a child. I am not worried."

Springheart followed her to where Willowvine was struggling against the ropes. "You will hurt yourself on that. My husband doesn't make mistakes when he ties a knot."

"My friends will need me," Willowvine answered.

Madeline knelt beside her. "I would like to be able to allow you some freedom. Will you take an oath that we are in no danger from you, and that you will not run away until we release the oath?"

Willowvine narrowed her eyes. She was weighing her options. "It would be better than this," she finally answered. "I'll take your oath, but you must promise that you will not take me away from here without my agreement."

Madeline nodded, and Springheart walked them through the oath. When the ropes were untied, Willowvine excused herself and disappeared behind a bush at the edge of the camp.

"Let's hope we don't come to regret this," Springheart said.

17

The next morning, Regis was strong enough to ride. Jode settled him into the saddle and added a few straps to stop him from falling. They tested Willowvine's oath by having one of the guards try to take her beyond the bounds. Madeline felt a headache growing the farther the girl went. At the very edge of her range, Willowvine's knees buckled.

"Bring her back," Madeline called. "She can ride with me in the wagon."

Amberbirch stepped beside the wagon and whispered, "She can ride with one of the men. Having her too close to you is dangerous. For your children, as well as the prophecy."

Madeline motioned for Willowvine to sit on the wagon bench. "I would prefer not to chance the effects of the oath should someone's horse bolt. I am capable of defending myself if the oath should break."

"As you wish," Amberbirch said curtly. "I am only thinking of your safety."

Unsettled at Amberbirch's clear jealousy of Willowvine, Madeline didn't respond. Instead she helped settle the girl on the bench beside her. "Will you conceal our camp?" she asked Amberbirch when they were done.

The woman stalked over and scattered herbs around the camp, providing a conceal spell to increase the odds that it would be there when they needed it. "If we are being observed, then they know where to find our belongings regardless of the spell," she said returning to her horse.

"We can spend a cold night on the ground if need be," Madeline said. "Willowvine's friends have little enough. If they take our supplies, we will survive."

Amberbirch's eyes narrowed at that, but she didn't speak. Madeline realized that she would be glad to leave the elves to their own prejudices when they returned home. "How far to the center of the valley?" she asked.

"At this pace, we will arrive in the late afternoon, perhaps a little closer to evening," Springheart said. "If we move faster, we are risking Regis' health."

Madeline wasn't willing to endanger any of them for the sake of her impatience. She was certain that they still had plenty of time to seal the gate, even if there was still a puzzle at the end of this journey. "Let's see how we feel after stopping for lunch."

THE AFTERNOON PACE favored safety over speed. Madeline tried to get information out of Willowvine as the day progressed, but all the girl said was, "You may be able to keep me with you, but your oath does not force me to tell you my life story."

As they neared their destination, Madeline was itching to push the group to a gallop, knowing it would be hard on the wagon wasn't enough to damp her urge for speed. Jode rode close to Regis to ensure that he would not fall under the hooves of the rest of the horses. Amberbirch seemed to be in a sulk, and the guards were too busy keeping them safe to chat.

"It makes for a long day," Springheart said pulling his horse alongside the wagon. "This silence is draining on the will."

"It does feel like there's a pall over our group. Perhaps it's because we are almost done." She hoped that it was true.

"It would be nice to think so," Springheart said. He leaned over and spoke to Willowvine. "Stop trying to think of ways to escape. We will release you when we leave."

Madeline felt the girl sit straighter. "What is this quest you are on? Why did you come here to my home?"

Springheart told the girl the story. "So, you can see why we cannot allow you to gather your gang again."

Willowvine didn't answer, and Madeline wondered if the quest had made a difference in her desire to break free. She worried that she hadn't noticed the girl was trying to escape.

They continued in silence until Amberbirch told them to stop. "We are here."

They dismounted, and Madeline stood at the edge of the trees. Before her was a perfect circle of clear grass. That was the only indication it had been created by anyone other than nature. The center of the clearing contained a stone pillar about four feet high. It seemed to echo the well, as though the stones that created it were the same as the stones within the well.

She felt someone stand beside her. Willowvine touched her arm, bringing Madeline out of her thoughts. Turning, she saw that the others were waiting in a line, the guards vigilant behind them.

"What do you see?" the girl asked. When Madeline didn't answer, she asked again, "Lady, they are all waiting for you. I'm waiting for you to get this done so I can be freed."

Madeline glanced at the center of the clearing. "What do you see, Willowvine?"

The girl made a noise of impatience and said, "Trees. I don't know why that woman said we were here. It looks like more of the same trees to me."

Madeline turned to see puzzled faces on everyone except Amberbirch. "How do you know we are at the center, Amberbirch?"

The woman stepped forward but stopped a few feet away. "We all see different things here. I see that the trees are different. They are older, but I still see only trees. If you can see something else, then we are where we need to be."

Madeline told them about the tower. "I don't know what you will observe when I go, but I'm going to the circle alone."

She could tell they didn't like it, but she didn't let them argue.

Willowvine grabbed her arm. "How far are you going? The oath…"

Madeline swore in frustration. Would there ever be a time when she could make a decision without complication? "It looks like it is close enough." She turned to check the clearing. She couldn't be sure that it wasn't at the very edge of the range for the oath. "Damn, I need to have a clear head for this."

The girl brightened. "Okay, just release the oath, and I'll be going."

"No, I can't be worried what you'll do when I'm in there. You are coming with me." She pulled the translation sheet from her bag, along with a few sheets of blank paper and a pen. "Maybe you can be helpful."

Madeline ran to give Jode a kiss. "Don't follow. We'll be fine."

He hugged her. "We will be here when you return."

Madeline waved to the others before taking Willowvine's hand and striding toward the clearing. "Is what you see changing?"

She felt the girl twitching. "No. As far as I can tell you are just dragging me through the trees, but I never seem to get hit. So, they are probably just an illusion."

When she reached the center, Madeline made the girl sit on the grass. "I'm going to read the words on the stone, can you write them down for me?"

Willowvine took the paper and pen. "Yes, I can write. We teach each other. And I wasn't born an orphan. I knew my parents."

Madeline didn't react to the information. She seemed to be attracting elven orphans. There would be time to hear the girl's story on the way back to the camp. That is if Willowvine wanted to tell it.

Walking to the stone column, Madeline circled it. It was created out of slabs of black stones carved and inlaid with silver to create the words. Twined within the message, Madeline saw a path of brighter silver flow from stone to stone. She held up the translation sheet and read the words aloud. "To seal the gate a sacrifice is needed. The Chosen will have a choice." The message ended. "That's not helpful," Madeline murmured. She walked back to Willowvine who was waiting, pen in hand.

"There must be more," the girl said. Her rebellious need to be free lost in what seemed to be curiosity. "How did you know this was the message?"

Madeline explained about the brighter words.

"Go back and see if there's another message. I've heard about this kind of thing. My mother was always trying to make some sense of ancient stuff. Sometimes the answer comes in layers. I've never heard of a message that was hidden that didn't eventually give an answer."

Madeline wondered at the type of society that would cast out such intelligent people. She returned to the column and saw that the girl was right. The first part of the message was a brighter silver, the second part, a darker silver. "The sacrifice that seals the gate for eternity will come from one without ties. The sacrifice that seals the gate for a thousand years will come from that which is of value to The Chosen."

It seemed like that was a complete answer, but Madeline walked around the column holding the translation sheet up to the words until she was sure that she hadn't missed anything.

They returned to the others and read the message. When she finished, Madeline looked over her shoulder and saw only trees. "I don't care if we have to travel in the dark, let's start for home."

"We're done," Willowvine said. "I want you to release me from the oath."

"Are you sure you don't want to stay with us until we get back to camp?" Springheart asked. "This is a long way from your friends."

She glared at him. "You said you would release me when we were done."

"Yes, that's what I promised," Madeline assured the girl. "Let's join the others first." When they were back together, Madeline asked how to release the oath. Following Springheart's instructions, she ended with, "There, you are free."

"Thank you. Now let's get going." Willowvine climbed into the wagon.

---

18

*T*he journey back to the camp went faster than the journey out. Regis agreed to ride behind Springheart which allowed them to move faster.

At the camp, Madeline stared at the mess. Someone had broken through the conceal spell. The only evidence that this was their campsite was the burned ground where their fire had been. "Your friends?" Madeline asked Willowvine. "How could they get through the spell?"

The elven girl knelt and ran her fingers across the ground. "Not my friends. Something else is here." She looked up at Madeline fear and accusation in her eyes. "What did you bring here? What have you exposed my clan to?"

Amberbirch joined them, placing her own hands on the dirt. "I think she is right. This doesn't smell of elf."

Madeline spun around as if the person who had destroyed their camp was lurking. "I didn't know anyone was following us. Jode, can you track them?"

He walked around the camp with Springheart, crouching to look for clues. The guards and Regis surrounded the women, swords drawn. Madeline felt as though someone was watching from the edge of the trees. "It's the other," she said with the overwhelming certainty of her magic. "The one who will open the gate forever. If they get there before us, they'll destroy everything." Panic crawled at the edge of her consciousness beating through her efforts to calm it. "We need to get back to the library."

"No, we need to find this person before they kill the world," Regis said. "Can you do that spell? The one that takes you back in time?"

Madeline nodded. "I need a minute." She stepped to the center of the circle and closed her eyes. This was going to take a lot of calming thoughts. "Everyone be quiet, please."

She sat and pictured the beach that calmed her. The grains of sand, the sound of the waves, the feel of the warm sun, the tang of salt in the air. When she felt the world slip away, Madeline focused on finding the image of events in the last day.

Shadows flickered into sight. Willowvine's friends searched through the mess of their campsite. Madeline watched as they found the food and blankets that were hidden. She was glad that at least someone benefited from the attack. When the spell started again, it slipped back to the day they left.

She saw the Scree appear at the edge of the camp. He was alone, which was unusual. He sniffed the air and then scattered white chalk around in a circle, making the camp appear. He rifled through their belongings. Tossing things aside as he realized there was nothing there.

When there was nothing left undisturbed, he strode away. Madeline waited until she was sure of his direction. He was moving away from the place where she'd found the message. Letting go of the trance, she returned to the present.

She told the others what she'd seen. "Unless there is a different location for a message to keep the gate open, he's not going to find his target."

"Why wouldn't there be a separate place?" Willowvine asked.

"If you had to go to the same places to find the clues, you could run into each other. Then you could fight, and we would know who won. And we would know our fate."

Madeline would have preferred to keep her more optimistic version. "Why are you still here?"

"I wanted to see what you would do. Maybe I'll hang around until you fix this problem." The girl's face didn't reflect the sass of her words. Madeline realized that Willowvine was feeling part of a family, and she didn't want to let it go.

"You can stay with us," Madeline said before rising. "Let's get back to the library. I know you are tired, but we'll be better off there. Maybe we'll figure out what to do and seal the gate in the next day or two. Then we don't need to worry about the Scree."

No one argued. They mounted up and rode for the library.

AT THE LIBRARY, they handed their horses to the servants to be stabled. Madeline would have enjoyed the peace of tending to the wagon horses, but the presence of the Scree had shortened their already scarce time. She couldn't indulge her own desires.

She strode into the room where the others were waiting. "We need to find the answer to these two choices," she said as she slumped on the couch. "I think we should go for the easiest choice. I'll toss something of value into the well, and we're done for a thousand years."

Amberbirch took a tray from the servant. She passed tea to everyone before sitting at the table with the model. "Are you sure that you know what you'll toss? Are you sure that the choice will be yours?"

The words were quiet, but they caught everyone's attention. Madeline looked around the room. Regis was falling asleep in a chair, Jode looked as though he was only staying awake by sheer will. Only the elves looked as alert as she felt. The questions deflated her confidence. "And what if it's not just a matter of throwing something down the well?" she asked the question that Amberbirch hadn't asked.

Willowvine looked to the two women. "Is there any other clue?" When they shook their heads, she added, "Then we must have the answer. I think we need to go to this circle. Now that we have this answer, perhaps the rest of the information will come."

"She is wise," Springheart said. "We are all tired. No matter how fast this Scree works, we have a few days at least. I suggest we rest and start again tomorrow."

"We can't stop. The answer is here, I know it is," Madeline's temper pressed at the rags of her patience. She'd struggled with gathering the information and now, when a Scree was stalking them, everyone just wanted to stop. "I don't know how much time we have. The presence of the Scree might change everything. We really have to…" she stopped speaking when she couldn't think of how to end the sentence. Her determination to keep going was losing ground to her fatigue. "It feels like we are on the edge of a cliff, and an earthquake is coming."

Jode reached for her. "We are all tired. Remember you are expending energy growing our children." He patted the mound of her pregnancy and one of the twins kicked at him. "They are probably taking more than their share. Rest will reveal more secrets than fretting. We are not stopping for more than a few hours. I promise."

Madeline didn't want to stop, but as she tried to think of an argument for staying up, weariness drowned her. "Fine, but we are going to the circle tomorrow. And at first light."

No one argued, but she wasn't sure if that was just a sign they were too weary to continue, or whether they agreed with her fears.

Despite the desperate need for sleep, Madeline's mind circled the things she knew about the prophecy as she curled against Jode in their small bed. As much as she didn't like to leave a job unfinished, she still felt that the option to seal it for a thousand years gave them time to find a permanent solution.

If she could only be sure that she understood what the messages meant, she would know what to do. If she could get rid of this horrible feeling that it would only be after they had tried everything that they would know that they had done the right thing.

19

*S*pringheart rose before the sun. In the time before the world knew day, but there was light. He'd been lying on the bed awake for hours, hoping to fall asleep, but not able to let go of mounting fears that this would turn out to be a disaster.

He stood at the window in the workroom watching the world fade into being as the light strengthened.

"Do you think it means us?" Willowvine's voice broke his attention.

He turned to answer her and saw how young she really was. She must have been a toddler when she lost her family. It was lucky for her that the bandits had taken her in.

When he didn't answer, she continued, "The ones without ties? Do you think it means us?"

He had wondered that same thing. "What makes you think it's not just someone without obligations? Someone who could sacrifice without implications on our world?"

She stepped forward to join him at the window, pulling a blanket around her shoulders. "Because elves wrote it and we all know what the others, the ones with families, think of us."

He turned to sit on the sill. "I have learned to assume nothing.

We think, no we believe, it was written by elves, but all that we know is that it is in the elven language. Perhaps this was a joint effort by all the beings of the first opening."

"Yes, elves. This was our world, there were no others until the gate opened."

He sought for words to comfort her. She could be right. If it was true, being sad until the last moment would not be the right emotion to feel. "Yes, and when the well was lined and the stones created, there were at least two species here. Whoever came first and the elves."

She sighed but seemed unwilling to argue. "Tell me about Madeline. She is not of our world, is she?"

"What makes you say that?" Springheart realized that he didn't know anything about the girl.

She leaned on the sill and watched as the first sliver of the sun crested the horizon. "I have magic that helps me identify danger. Everyone here has an aura of good and bad. Some are more bad than others, but Madeline has no aura. She doesn't shine either way."

Springheart knew the facts, but that was only one flavor of the story, and Willowvine wanted more that the facts he'd given her a day ago. "You should ask her about it," he said eventually. "Do you smell that? I believe the servants are preparing breakfast. Come, let's eat. Everyone will eventually join us."

"Wait. Why didn't you ask what your aura says about you?" The girl clearly didn't realize that it would have been an intrusion. Being raised by bandits gave her the advantage of directness.

Springheart bowed. "It would be impertinent. If you wish to tell me, then I am happy to hear."

She turned back to the window. "You're mostly good. But there's something else. When I look at each individual, I see the normal mix of good and bad. Like I said, everyone has both. But..."

Springheart waited out the pause. Willowvine was struggling with something. She rubbed her temples after a few minutes. "It's not just people I can see. It's a group. With the bandits, I mostly saw them balanced as bad. They would do anything to survive – maybe I would have too. But when I looked at the group aura, I would see good. We looked out for each other."

"They became your family," he said. "When you return will they accept you back?"

She shrugged. "I don't know if I'm going to return. I'm old enough now to find my way. Maybe I'll do what you did."

"I am happy to help you find work in the world," he said.

"Thanks, but let's leave that until after." She took a deep breath and then the words came out in a rush, "When I look at this group aura, I see something dark. Not bad exactly, just dark. I can't see who is making it happen. I've never seen this before."

Springheart looked over his shoulder to ensure they were alone. "Perhaps it is because of the weight of our task."

Willowvine considered it for only a second. "No, I've seen that before. This is an absence. It's like the group is missing a member."

Springheart watched the emotions flash across Willowvine's face. A frown of frustration, then sigh of defeat. "We are waiting for Madeline's teacher to arrive. It is possible that is the absence you see."

She ran her fingers through her hair. "Maybe. There was one more thing. Something I've seen before. Vengeance. Someone in this group wants vengeance for something, and they won't care what Madeline chooses. If they don't get their revenge, they will do something dangerous."

Springheart led Willowvine away from the door. They could not be overheard for this. "Most of us have reason to want revenge for something. I cannot imagine that any of these reasons is enough to risk destroying us."

"Maybe they don't see it that way. Sometimes people look at

their actions differently. Like why would the Scree want the gate open? They are in as much danger as everyone else." Willowvine looked to Springheart as if he had all the knowledge she needed.

He couldn't answer the question she posed. "Why do Scree do anything? I think that we must keep this between us, Willowvine. I will only tell Madeline. We will find the answer before it is too late."

20

Frustrated at the delay, Madeline stood at the window. She'd tried to argue for them to leave for the gate immediately, but none of the others had agreed with her. The argument that finally won her over was that she didn't yet know what to do when the choice was made. If there was more information in the library, she would need to be there to find it. The only thing at the gate, was the gate. She didn't like the fact that their logic won out over her instinct, but she also knew they were right. No matter how much time they had, it wasn't enough to keep running to the gate every time she felt the pull.

Trying to decide what she would be willing to sacrifice, if she even had the choice, was tearing at her. There was not going to be an easy way out. Whatever happened, she would feel the loss of someone. The choice of sacrificing someone with no ties was not an option as far as she was concerned. Sacrificing something for a thousand years of safety was the choice. No matter who it turned out to be, she would not consider sacrificing anyone. She ignored the feeling that her preferences were not going to matter.

"Madeline, may I talk with you?" Springheart's voice cut through her thoughts.

She invited him to take a seat. Any interruption of this useless circling between one unanswerable question and another was welcome.

"I need to tell you something. It is something Willowvine has learned," he said quietly.

"Why can't she tell me herself?" Madeline hated secondhand information.

"I think this is something you need to hear from a friend. If you wish to, I'm sure she will talk to you."

Madeline ignored her first reaction, which was to say she wouldn't listen to rumors. This wasn't some petty office politics; this was life or death. "Tell me and we'll see."

Springheart shared what Willowvine had told him. "I can only hope that Blu is the missing person," he finished, adding no opinion on who might be seeking revenge.

Madeline really wanted to kick something. Every time she thought they had found the last obstacle, something else popped up to bar her way to a quiet and peaceful life. Her anger disturbed the twins who started kicking, and that gave her heartburn. She knew that she'd been lucky so far with the effects of pregnancy, but now every day something new happened with that. If she couldn't keep her body healthy enough, would that affect the sealing?

Patting her belly to calm the children, Madeline tried to keep the anger out of her tone. "Who has reason to want vengeance?" Maybe they could find and neutralize the problem.

Springheart flushed, and Madeline wondered if her words had been too blunt. "I'm sorry, Springheart, we don't have time for niceties."

He stood and started pacing the room. "No, it is not that. Your question hit my own conscience. I think we all have reason for it, but not all reasons for revenge result in actions."

Once more, Madeline wished that Blu was with them. His wisdom was something she missed sorely. If he didn't have an answer, at least he would have better questions. Then she remembered that he rarely gave answers. "Tell me. Knowing the reasons might help us determine the person."

He stopped pacing and rejoined her. "I do not know what your reasons would be, but of the elves here, I would think Willowvine is the least likely to be our problem. She did not need to tell me of this if it were her."

Madeline knew that it wasn't necessarily true. She'd seen enough sabotage in the form of friendly advice to know that there was a possibility for the girl to be undermining them for some reason. "That holds true for you as well."

"I have many reasons to want revenge for my treatment. But that is the way of my people. If being outcast was reason to risk the whole world, you would not have to look far for the culprit." He rose again as though sitting made the problem worse, and by pacing he could find a solution. "I do not think that the servants will have the opportunity to act against you. It must be one of us five."

Madeline agreed with his logic but kept the thought to herself. "I have no reason for sabotaging us. In fact, I have every reason to make this work." She patted her belly unconsciously. "Jode would not act against me even if he had reason." She hoped that was true. While you never really knew another person, Jode didn't seem to have a vengeful bone in his body. "Regis had the opportunity to let me die. And Amberbirch has always been there to help us find the answers. Without her creating the translation sheet, I would never have found the clues."

Springheart stopped his pacing again and turned to her. "You have reasons for everyone to be innocent, but it must be one of us."

She saw the fear on his face. He thought she wasn't taking it seriously. "I will keep in mind that we may have a traitor in our midst. It may be that Willowvine is seeing something other than vengeance. Perhaps it is the presence of the Scree? Perhaps she is feeling out of place here."

He seemed to consider the possibility that Willowvine had been wrong. "Her magic is different from mine, different from most elves. There is no question when I use it. A wound or sickness is healed. Her magic is more like yours. Perhaps you understand more than I do."

"If it is like my prescient magic, then we cannot rely on understanding the message until it is too late. I only know that something important will happen. I don't even know if it is a bad thing, or good."

"I hope that is not true of Willowvine. The consequences are too grave to wait until after the damage is done," he said.

Madeline was tired of the discussion. She knew this was important, but had learned that chasing a warning without proof was a waste of time, and time was the thing they had very little to waste. "Don't tell anyone else. I promise I will keep this in mind as we proceed. But, Springheart, there is another reading of what she saw. The vengeance may help us seal the gate. The emotion behind the act isn't always going to result in failure. Perhaps we all have different reasons to wish this threat gone, but that doesn't mean we will fail."

"You are The Chosen One. Perhaps you have more understanding." His words were snapped out.

"Yes. Everyone says that, but no one seems willing to listen to me." Madeline regretted her bitterness as the words left her. Springheart was only trying to help, and she'd just dismissed him the way the other elves did.

She saw the disbelief cross his face as he paled. Her words hadn't rung true to her ears either, but she needed them all focused on the main goal. They needed to understand what it was going to take to seal the gate, whether for a thousand years, or forever. They didn't have the answer yet. And she would not be held at the library for much longer.

21

*S*pringheart left the room feeling unsatisfied with the outcome of his meeting with Madeline. Everything she'd said was true, but he had a feeling deep inside that what Willowvine had told him was important. Not wanting to meet anyone, he left the library to stroll. The woods surrounding the building were thick enough to hide it after only a few steps. Springheart stayed off the path. If they needed him, he would be harder to find that way.

Knowing that Madeline would want to make the journey to the well as soon as she could, Springheart thought he could delay by not being there. He didn't expect it to work for very long. She would be more likely to tell him to follow if he wasn't there, than wait.

He reached the lake in a few minutes by creating his own path. It was a place of solitude and healing for him, the sun turned the surface of the lake into a silver mirror. Ripples from the breeze made the light dance on its surface. The boulders were warm and welcoming. Only the sound of insects broke the peace, but those sounds were soporific rather than irritating.

He folded himself into a meditation position. If he could find some wisdom in the calm of a trance, perhaps he could find some proof for Madeline. With proof, perhaps she would be more able to take the right course of action.

Slipping easily into his trance, Springheart began to examine everything he'd learned.

"Sorry, I thought no one would be here," Regis' voice broke through the peace of Springheart's meditation.

Letting go, Springheart welcomed Regis. If fate was not willing to allow him time to meditate, then perhaps it had sent him someone to talk with. "You came here for a reason?"

Regis nodded and folded into a cross legged position. "The library is in a bit of turmoil. Madeline is determined to take these last steps toward the end in the next ten minutes. I needed a place to try to reach out to Blu. I thought perhaps he would have some words to calm this tempest that has stirred her."

Springheart worried that his news had made things worse. "Do not let my presence stop you."

Regis closed his eyes. As he formed the spell, Springheart watched his friend's lips move in silent conversation. This was a good sign, perhaps Regis had been right. The exchange only lasted a few minutes before Regis nodded and opened his eyes. "They are only two days out. Perhaps that will calm Madeline." He stretched and stared out over the water. "It is beautiful here, but I am looking forward to seeing the Summer Lands."

"It will become your home," Springheart said. "Home will always be the most beautiful place."

"We'll see. I think Arabela might need some convincing that I belong there." He turned to face Springheart. "Why did you come here?"

Madeline had asked Springheart to keep his news from the others, but he had agreed to nothing. Regis had proven himself on the journey. The anger and vengeance he'd displayed in The City was gone, had been gone for months. Springheart dearly needed to talk to someone, and his request to Willowvine to keep it secret had been more about her not speaking of it than him. He told Regis what he'd learned and how Madeline had reacted.

"And you think she's wrong," Regis said.

Springheart didn't want to think about it that way, but Regis had read him correctly. "I feel as if we are being told that there will be consequences if we allow the gate to be sealed with hatred in our hearts. I know that sounds insane, but I think we are better knowing the motives of our companions, than we are pretending we are all saints."

Regis walked to the edge of the water and picked up a handful of pebbles. He skipped the first stone before saying, "Okay, so what do you think we need to do about it?"

The question caught Springheart unawares. His focus had been only on the problem. Perhaps that's why he had been unable to see any way out. "If we can convince Madeline that there is a danger, she will act."

Regis tossed the last of his pebbles. "No, I think we need more. If you trust me, then you don't think I am the danger. You aren't, or you wouldn't bring up the subject. You can't think Madeline is..." Regis stopped. A frown crossed his face. "Do you think it might be her?"

"How could it be her?" Springheart felt the answer rise from the deepest part of his mind as he asked. "She has much to be angry about. She was taken from her world. She has been doing everyone's bidding since. It is possible that the vengeful one isn't aware of it."

Regis shrugged. "I think we can only rely on guesses, but that doesn't mean we won't guess right. You want Madeline to acknowledge there's a problem, right? Then that's all we need to do. Even if we could find out who it was, they might be critical to our success."

Springheart rose and brushed dirt from his pants. "I think I have done everything I can. Madeline has the news, and she will not change her mind with more argument. If we are to change her mind, we need to find the reason for this vengeance. When the priest arrives, he may be able to help. In the meantime, I will ask Willowvine to try to find the source of this aura."

When they arrived back at the library, Springheart heard Madeline calling for her husband to pack books for the trip to the gate. He left Regis to pass on the news from Blu and went to find Willowvine. The girl may yet not be able to focus her magic, but if she were trained, that might change.

He found her curled up on one of the benches outside. There was a plate on the ground beside her, only a crust of bread and core of an apple remained. He wondered if she'd ever had food available at request in her life. Living in the hills with bandits would have been his fate, if the elders hadn't needed someone to run messages. He knew that he was fortunate not to have been cast out when his mother died. It was rare, but when there was value to be found, the elves with no family were kept within the tribe, not welcomed, kept.

The girl was sleeping and Springheart left her there. A few hours would make no difference, and she deserved to feel safe enough to sleep for a little while.

---

22

*A*fter Springheart left, Madeline realized that she was starting to spin in circles. She needed Simon. He was the only person in this world she didn't have to worry about getting her meaning rather than the literal words. He was also someone she trusted enough to not undermine what she had to do. Everyone from this world had an agenda that Madeline couldn't understand, would never truly understand. And despite her saying it might not matter, she knew full well that the end didn't justify the means. Even if this person was working with her, the vengeance would taint the results.

She decided that she would talk with Willowvine later. Maybe they would be able to identify the culprit together. She hoped with all her heart that the person didn't turn out to be someone vital to their success. Madeline pushed aside all thoughts of identifying the person, knowing that inventorying everyone and trying to figure out what they were hiding, wouldn't move her forward.

She needed to sort out what she would be willing to sacrifice so that the gate could be sealed.

Jode entered, interrupting her thoughts with his mere presence. "Has something happened?" she asked.

He sat beside her and brushed her hair off her face. "Why must something have happened? I thought that you might need someone to talk to."

"The last person who tried to talk to me left the room before we could finish our discussion," she said ruefully.

"Not just the room." He laughed. "Springheart has left the library; by the look on his face, he will be gone for a while. Regis has also taken a walk. The child sleeps, and Amberbirch plans to visit the village. We are alone."

"It feels like everyone has left so that I cannot make the journey to the well. Are they forcing me to cool down?"

He led her to the couch. "Let's get some rest ourselves. I know it is early, but a nap may refresh your mind more than just worrying over the problems you face. I think that each of them has need for solitude, the fact that you will have to wait a day before rushing off to the gate is a side benefit."

Madeline curled up beside her husband. She didn't feel the need for sleep, but taking a break might give her some perspective. "What do you think I should do?"

He kissed her and then started stroking her hair. Madeline felt the tension ebb as he soothed her. "Do? Which of your monumental tasks are you referring to?"

She snuggled in closer and turned her face to look into his eyes. "The prophecy. Which choice should I take?"

He didn't speak for several minutes. Madeline felt drowsiness wrap around her and was succumbing to sleep when Jode finally spoke. "I think that is the wrong question. I wonder if you are considering the whole problem. You know that there are two outcomes, and that each will require a sacrifice."

Madeline nodded. She kept Willowvine's vision to herself. "I've been trying to think what I value enough to use as the sacrifice. I think it will have to be something big to do such big magic, but it will be a thing, not a person."

Jode moved his hand to her belly, receiving a kick from one of the twins, one so hard it made Madeline grunt. "These children are anxious to be noticed," he said. "Perhaps they have your answer."

Laughing, Madeline placed her hand over his. "If I thought that was possible, I'd be trying to talk to them." She shifted to sit more upright without breaking his embrace. "I have so little to sacrifice. I would give the spell our lands, or any of the jewels that you've given me, but I don't think that's what we need."

He shook his head. "It will be something that is part of you. What if you have to give it your ability to feel joy, or love?"

Madeline hadn't thought in such abstract terms. Would she relinquish her love for Jode? Yes, to save Cartref, she would give away the feeling. Knowing that she loved him and being loved in return would be enough. "I know that I won't willingly sacrifice anyone I know. I think it will demand Springheart, or Willowvine, or both. The spell is elven, so it will be interpreted through their values. I will not send either of them down that well."

"Have you considered that the choice should be theirs?" Jode shook his head when Madeline started to answer. "You do not need to argue with me. I just ask that you consider that you are taking away their ability to fulfill their destiny. And for them the sacrifice might be worth the result. To never face another enemy invading from the gate, is a strong incentive."

Madeline pulled away from Jode. Looking at the peaceful scene through the window, she told him what Willowvine had seen. "So, I can't leave it up to them. What if this vengeful person is just waiting to be the sacrifice? And the prophecy said I had to make the choice."

He rose to stand beside her. "Perhaps that is true. How will you decide?"

"I have to go to the circle," she answered. "I know you don't want me to, but that's where the answers will be. That's where we have to go to make this choice."

"Then we will go, tomorrow," Jode said. "Today we must rest. Yours is not the only temper that is easily sparked. Let us take today to rest and make peace. If we are fortunate, tomorrow we will find the answer."

Madeline sighed. "I've thought that so many times, I'm beginning to wonder if there is a final answer."

He kissed her again. "I have every confidence that you will find the solution. Even if the final one is withheld until the moment of the ceremony. You are The Chosen after all."

She laughed. "I'll take that as comfort. Look, here come Springheart and Regis. I should start by making amends with Springheart. Then I'll talk to Willowvine myself."

Madeline found Springheart as he crept away from the sleeping elven child. "She seems to be far away from here. I envy her the ability to sleep so soundly," Madeline said.

"I am certain she will wake at the slightest indication of danger. You do not live long as a bandit by ignoring the world around you." He gave one more glance at the child.

"True, but she's sleeping now." Madeline beckoned him into the kitchen. "I want to apologize for my behavior."

Springheart dismissed her words. "It is the stress. We are all wound tightly. Let us say no more about it."

Madeline took him at his word. "We go to the gate tomorrow. I think our answers are there."

"You may be right," he said. "We have news of your priest. He is only two days away."

Feeling like there was hope in the news, Madeline smiled. "Then we will need to return to the library for the evening. Am I a coward for being relieved at having an excuse to avoid sleeping near that hole in the ground?"

"You are far from a coward, Madeline," Springheart assured her.

23

*S*pringheart walked away from Madeline, leaving her to the task of organizing the trip to the circle. Although it would be a short trip tomorrow, Madeline seemed determined to take every resource that might help her to solve the latest conundrum. He couldn't put aside the feeling that there was something to Willowvine's vision, and that there was no way the vengeance could be beneficial to their group.

If, at the last minute, someone were to interfere, no matter what Madeline decided to do, it could result in disaster. It could result in the opposite of what she intended. He needed to find a way to pinpoint the person, even if not the motivation.

He sought out Willowvine and found her in the temporary garden the cook had placed near the back of the library. She was kneeling and inhaling the aromas of the herbs. There was something delicate in the way she touched the plants, more a caress then a handling. It was as though the plants willingly shared their bounty with her.

He stepped on the pebbles that bordered the garden, deliberately scattering a few to make noise. She turned, startled despite his care, reaching for a knife that was not on her hip.

"You were almost dead," she said laughing and walked toward him. "I knew there was a reason you made me disarm when we arrived."

"You looked like you were enjoying yourself." He took her arm and drew her to a seat that was placed at the edge of the garden. Even in something as prosaic as a temporary herb garden, his people made sure there was beauty and a place of reflection. "I need to ask you about this taint you saw on our group."

"I haven't told anyone, like you asked," she said.

He reassured her that he trusted her before admitting that he'd shared the information with Regis and Madeline. "I have to believe that I can trust those two of our party."

"You want to find out who it is," she said. "You think you can do that with my magic."

She was perceptive, he admitted to himself. "There are only so many people it can be. I cannot do this truly by my own feelings. But I would ask that you help to eliminate as many of our party from the suspect list as possible."

Willowvine leaned back against the warmed stone of the bench. "I've never tried to do that. I've never had to. How should we do it?"

Springheart had been considering this since he'd spoken to Regis. He had a plan of sorts. "I think we cannot assume that you consider the party to comprise the same people I do, we do. Can we start by identifying the components of our list of suspects?" He held a hope that it was not one of their party. Perhaps one of the guards, or servants, were more than they seemed.

"I can sense people a long way out. It's like a circle I cast over everyone. I can sense out to a half day's walk in any direction. Do you want me to start with the wide search?"

He nodded, thinking it would be of value to know who was nearby since they had potential enemies in her old gang, and this mysterious wandering Scree.

She nudged him to stand. "It takes a lot of energy to go far. I think it will be better if I'm lying down. At least if I lose consciousness, I won't fall."

He stood and took the opportunity to keep watch. Interruptions would likely make this harder than it needed to be. Casting for enemies where he thought he had finally found friends left a bitter taste. One that he would tolerate in the name of saving the world.

Willowvine lay on her back, arms crossed over her chest, like a hero laid to rest. She breathed a deep sigh, and then closed her eyes. He watched her features relax as she entered a trance. Springheart observed as her breathing slowed, the color drained from her skin, and she seemed to relinquish her hold on life. He had not thought to ask what he should expect, so now he was feeling the edge of panic. Had something gone wrong? Should he try to rouse her? Would that do more damage? Was she dying?

Seconds passed like hours. Springheart focused on the rise and fall of the girl's chest. If she was still breathing, then she was alive.

Just as he made the decision to disturb her, Willowvine shuddered and gasped as though she were drowning. Color flooded her skin and she sat bolt upright. Springheart rushed to support her and felt the chill of her skin ebb as he wrapped her in his arms. "Are you all right? Is this normal."

She patted his arms, and then held on as she regained her control. Her gasping subsided to deep breaths and then to the cadence of regular breathing. "I'm fine. I don't know if it's normal. I've never done that before. I'm glad I did. That talent will come in handy the next time I have to know where guards are before I steal… I mean…"

He laughed and released her. "I have had to resort to taking things a time or two. Did you learn anything?" He hoped that she hadn't wasted the energy, and his fear.

"I think so," she said pulling herself to her feet. "I saw the

Scree and I cannot tell his intentions — well other than the fact that he is not our culprit."

"Why can't you?" Springheart asked, hoping the answer would help him to find another way to identify the vengeance seeker.

"It flickers, and I don't know how to read a Scree. I've never met one."

"Very well, we will try something else." He gestured to the kitchen. "You should probably eat."

She stood her ground. "Why would we try something else?"

Springheart frowned. Had she forgotten what they were doing? "To find our—"

"Culprit," she finished his statement. "If you let me finish, you'll know that I found something out about that too."

"Perhaps if you had started with that information, it would have helped." Even so, Springheart knew that he would not have waited to hear about the Scree. Thinking that the information was less vital than the original purpose for her trance.

"The aura is not here right now. It's that way." Willowvine pointed in the direction of the village.

"Amberbirch? Why would she…" Springheart's mind couldn't accept what he's heard. "She has been helping us this whole time. I don't understand why she would seek vengeance more than any of us."

Willowvine shrugged. "I don't have that kind of talent. Can we go find food now?"

H E L E F T her with the cooks, after making sure she wouldn't even hint at what they'd found. Walking away from the friendly chatter of the servants, Springheart found himself entering an old section of the library. This circular room contained the books that Madeline had determined were of no use. The records of the families of the elves. He had avoided this room because it gave a hard reminder of his lack of status. There was no book here that recorded his birth. Regardless of Springheart's existence, the elders would not make any other entries in his mother's book. And each year the elders culled the broken lines from the walls. No one knew when that happened. No one knew where those books were kept. His would have been pulled within a year of his birth.

Books lined the shelves three deep. The shelves lined the walls from floor to ceiling the height of three normal rooms. A ladder ran on a track around the room. The only break in the rows of shelves was the doorway. Light flooded the room from the glass dome. At night, the only light would come from candles. There was a spell of location carved into the stone behind the books. If there were a book for Springheart's family, it would have glowed for him. Since he was looking for another family's record, he had only to speak the name of a living member, and the book would push to the front of its shelf, standing out from its companions.

"Amberbirch," Springheart said. Then he scanned the shelves for the movement of the books. It must have been in one of the front rows because there was no noise of books moving position. He would need to search the shelves for one that stood higher, or more forward. The book could not be removed from this room, so it was only a matter of patience.

As the minutes passed, Springheart began to worry that Amberbirch would return and catch him. The books on the lower shelves were all perfectly aligned. He climbed the ladder that allowed access to the full height of the shelves. If Amberbirch had attempted to obscure her history, the book could be anywhere, but more logically it would be on a top shelf, out of the easy sight of most people.

He ran up to the top of the ladder and started moving it around the room, scanning as he went. There would be few reasons for her to hide her family history. Perhaps there was an incident she was ashamed of in her ancestry. Elves were not perfect, but as long as they had family, it's possible to find forgiveness. The only other reason she would have to hide it, was the cull. It wouldn't be hidden from the elders, but it would from causal inquiry.

Finding the book on a shelf a third of the way from the top, Springheart brought it to a table in the center of the room. The book indicated that Amberbirch had two children. A son and a daughter. The son had died in the war at the last opening of the gate. So many sons and daughters had died then, that it was no surprise hers was one of the dead, or that Amberbirch had pursued the research.

The daughter had been born a few years before the son died. She had pursued a career in diplomacy and the last update showed her acting as the ambassador to a kingdom of humans on the farthest of the outer islands.

24

Madeline checked her list. She knew that taking so much for a day visit must look like madness, but she didn't want to waste any time. Tomorrow they would leave at dawn and stay until she had an answer, or the well attacked them as it had before. Having the books on the list wouldn't slow them down as much as having to return to get something they'd missed.

She would check her plans with Amberbirch when the woman returned from the village. It would give her a chance to gauge Amberbirch's intent. Willowvine's vision was only causing the group to be suspicious. Although she knew that Amberbirch would have to be told what the girl saw, Madeline wanted her opinion on their plan before Amberbirch had a chance to share her suspicion of everyone. Trying to see the clues in the behavior of the people she once trusted completely was only making Madeline crazy. She vowed to stop doing it and concentrate only on actions that would result in closing the gate. After all, her own magic was silent on the subject. If she was not getting any warning, then it couldn't be that important.

She had finished the inventory of the books and other

supplies in the bed of the wagon when Springheart and Willowvine found her.

"Madeline, I think you need to hear what we've discovered," Springheart said.

She dusted her hands on the seat of her pants, trying to suppress her impatience before responding. It felt like she'd summoned them by choosing to ignore the subject. "You have something new? Something that tells me who is going to be a problem?"

Willowvine tried to turn and leave, but Springheart held her in place. Madeline hadn't meant to frighten the girl, and she was surprised that Willowvine could be put off with a few words.

"Yes, we have," Springheart said. "I think we should go somewhere more private for this discussion."

Madeline sighed, but checked her temper. She had done all she could to prepare, and she didn't think taking a rest was on the cards anyway; the kids were kicking, and her mind was spinning. "Fine, where do you propose?"

"My room is likely the best place," Springheart said. "You may want to share this with the others, but right now only Willowvine and I have the knowledge."

Madeline agreed and followed the two elves to the small room that Springheart used as a bedroom. Its original function was storage, so there were no windows, and the bed filled most of the space. Springheart gestured for the two women to sit on the bed while he leaned against the door. His presence would ensure that no one could intrude.

"Tell her what we found," he said to Willowvine.

Willowvine didn't preface her words. "It's Amberbirch."

Madeline sat back, unprepared for the identity. "Tell me from the beginning. I need to know how you came to this realization."

Springheart took over the story and told Madeline how they had identified Amberbirch as the vengeful one. "I have tried to find a reason why Amberbirch would feel this way. If we knew why, perhaps we could tell whether it's a problem."

Madeline was finding it hard to imagine the woman who had helped and guided them through the entire search would be plotting to undermine the success. "Is there any reason for someone to want the gate left open? I can't imagine that Amberbirch is willing to allow a war to happen for some kind of revenge."

"I don't know if the vengeance will make you fail," Willowvine said. She reached for Madeline's arm. "I only see the emotion."

"And I have magic that warns me of important events." She looked at Springheart. "I've had no warning. Why do you think this is going to make us fail?"

"I have no reason other than a feeling that we are ignoring something vital. That the elves who wrote the solution would not have made this so complicated. There is no reason for that. The Chosen is the trigger. Until you came there was no opportunity for someone to try to seal the gate."

Madeline stood. "It's possible that without the complexity, anyone could have tried and failed. Since we know that doing it the wrong way will result in the gate being open forever, I have no problem with this being convoluted." She silenced the little voice that called her a liar.

"Are you going to tell anyone about Amberbirch?" Willowvine asked.

Madeline shook her head. "I'm not going to tell anyone until I've talked to Amberbirch." Willowvine pulled away from her and started toward the door. "No, don't worry I won't let her know that you've identified her."

"If she knows it's me, she'll retaliate." The girl sounded frightened. "I've been on the receiving end of retaliation, and I'm not going to let it happen again."

"I won't let her hurt you," Springheart said. "If she tries, we will stop her, but you can rely on Madeline's discretion."

Madeline assured the girl that she would pretend she was

asking everyone the questions. They agreed on a plan that would have Springheart complain about being accused to put Amberbirch's suspicions to rest. "Now tell me about this Scree. I am curious about what you did learn even if you didn't sense his intentions."

Willowvine gave Madeline the details. "His aura was faint because he was so far away. It flickered, and I couldn't pin down one intention. I could try again."

"Later perhaps," Madeline said. "What was his aura flickering between?"

The girl shrugged. "At first, I thought it was between anger and pleasure, but it didn't seem right. Now that I've had time to think, I'm sure the emotions were fear and hope. What would a Scree fear?"

"Me." Madeline told the girl her history with Sayer Goddard and his family. "We thought there were no family members left to carry on the blood feud, but there were some distant cousins. You were there, Springheart. When I slew the boy Teeso, the feud ended. The remaining cousins were banished."

Springheart moved away from the door before speaking. "With Scree, you never know what they have in their hearts. I find it hard to believe this lone Scree would fear you and still be nearby."

"He's getting closer," Willowvine said quietly.

Madeline turned away from Springheart to see the girl collapse onto the bed, her skin white and her eyes fluttering closed.

Springheart ran to her side and checked the girl's temperature. "She needs rest and food. Will you stay while I bring a tray?"

Madeline nodded and motioned for him to hurry. She sat beside Willowvine on the bed and felt her skin. There was some heat despite the appearance of death. At her touch, the girl's eyes came open. "I saw this time. It is hope."

"Hush, you didn't need to do that. We have time." Madeline

took the blanket from the bottom of the bed and covered Willowvine.

"No, he is going to the gate," she whispered. "He will arrive tomorrow."

Madeline frowned. How did she know that? "Have you been to the gate?"

Willowvine blinked her eyes slowly, clearly struggling to stay awake. "No, but it has an aura. It is black and full of hate and anger and everything that is horrible."

Before Madeline could ask for more details, Willowvine slipped into sleep.

25

*A*mberbirch arrived back at the library just before dinner. Madeline pulled the woman aside to talk to her. She'd been thinking of how to approach the subject without even hinting at the source.

They met in the library room where Madeline had spent her months doing the research. There were fewer books now and the table was clear. The books were in the wagon waiting to be transported to the circle of stones. The papers Madeline had used to work out her puzzles were tidied into a pile which she planned to review tonight and on the journey. The benefit of being denied a horse was that she could more easily study in the wagon.

"Is the child ill?" Amberbirch asked when they were settled. "I can see to her if she needs me."

Madeline didn't like the thought of sending Amberbirch to help. Willowvine was more likely to react badly than to accept healing from someone she thought was a traitor. "No, I think she's just eaten more than she's used to and has a stomach ache. I'm sure she will learn her lesson, but it must be hard to see such plentiful food when you are used to thin rations."

Amberbirch eyed Madeline suspiciously before nodding. "What did you want to talk to me about?"

This was the tricky part. Madeline had decided to pretend she wanted the woman's help in identifying the potential traitor. Asking questions that would include Amberbirch's assessment of herself as a risk should work. It was like being in court. If you asked the right questions, people implicated themselves more often than not.

"Willowvine's vision has me worried. I don't know enough about everyone to feel like I can trust anyone." Madeline looked down at her hands, trying to send the impression that she wasn't capable of suspecting anyone. It worked so well that she almost believed it herself. "Do you know of any reason someone would want to sabotage us?"

Amberbirch pressed her lips together and thought. "In these circumstances, you are right, it is impossible to know even your own motivation. We all carry hidden desires that taint our actions."

Madeline nodded, encouraged by the answer. "I know I have no hidden agenda. I love this world, and all of my friends are here. I would do anything to save it."

"You are not angry about being taken from your world to save Lady Arabela's land?"

Madeline had no reservations about her answer, although she wondered if Amberbirch had just revealed how easily she would have felt such anger. "When I first came, I might have acted differently. But since I fell in love with Jode, I wouldn't go back for anything."

"Even if that was the sacrifice required to seal the gate?" Amberbirch watched Madeline closely.

She thought about the question. Would she go back? Yes. It was the same as giving her life and she would do that if it meant a permanent solution. In fact, the main reason she was willing to take the option to close the gate for a thousand years was her suspicion that her life was the sacrifice it required. Right now, sacrificing her life meant three lives, and she couldn't make that decision. "Yes, I would do that for Cartref. What about you? I can't believe you have a hidden agenda. Something lurking in your heart that would interfere with our task." Madeline laughed to add a level of disbelief to her words hoping to avoid raising the woman's suspicions.

Amberbirch rose and stood at the window, thinking for a few minutes before answering, "I have many things lurking within my heart. No one reaches my age without experiencing some slights. But there is nothing that would cause me to destroy my world. If I were The Chosen, I would sacrifice anything to seal that horror."

That felt like a door shutting to Madeline, and she couldn't think of how to reopen it without it seeming like an interrogation. She wasn't convinced of the danger, and, if there was any, she imagined it would be coming from the Scree who was likely working against them. "What about the others? Do you know any reason they would want to stop us from sealing the gate?"

Amberbirch rejoined Madeline at the table. "I only know Springheart well enough to answer that question." She paused and seemed to be struggling internally with her answer. "I am not comfortable with gossip, but this situation is so serious that I feel compelled to answer."

Madeline had heard that statement from other people in the past. It generally preceded a solid backstabbing. She couldn't ignore any information the woman was willing to share, no matter how distasteful the source. If she was wrong, and the enemy was within their group, then Madeline needed to know. Her suspicions of Amberbirch faded as she said, "I will not betray your confidence."

Gathering her robe around her, Amberbirch lowered her voice, "This comes from when Springheart learned that he would never be part of the Elven world. He vowed that we would regret the choice we made."

"Wasn't he a child?" Madeline knew that Springheart worked for the elves as a courier. Why would they entrust him with that if he was considered a risk?

"Yes, that is why no one was concerned. But sometimes people hide their anger to make it possible to enact revenge." Amberbirch rose. "I think that dinner is ready, Madeline. Will you come?"

Madeline was still trying to absorb the information. "I will be along shortly. I need a few minutes."

She watched as Amberbirch left the room before trying to make sense of the woman's words. Holding a grudge for so long would surely be impossible. Wouldn't Springheart show some signs of his need for revenge? He'd always seemed resigned to his status, more he seemed to accept it. But perhaps that was part of his cover up. There had always been stories of spies being in place for decades. Moles who lived and thrived in enemy territory until they could set off the bomb or get the important secret. Was that what Springheart was doing? Seeming to be helpful while planning their downfall.

Madeline groaned. She was not used to things being so muddled. In the past, she either knew what to do, or had no clue. This wavering between understanding and confusion was almost as wearing as fighting a battle.

"Madeline it's late," Jode said as he strolled into the room. "You need to eat and rest. Do you forget that you are pregnant?" He held out his hand to help her rise.

"I'll rest when we are done, I promise. I have so much to think about. I don't know if I can sleep."

He led her to their room where Madeline saw a platter of food. "I thought we deserved an evening alone. It feels as though I am constantly searching for you, and when I find you, there is another crisis to resolve."

Madeline shrugged out of her clothes into the nightdress that was laid on the bed. Her pregnancy was getting bigger every day. She rubbed the bump, well it was no longer a bump, twins needed room. "This time isn't any different. I've had bad news all day – well, except for the news that Blu will be here the day after tomorrow." She made a sandwich from the contents of the platter and took it to eat on the bed. Madeline told Jode what she'd learned about Willowvine's vision. "So, I am not to trust someone, but I am not sure who."

Jode joined her in the bed, his own sandwich in his hand. "I think you do know who you will not trust." He looked at her as he chewed. "You don't want to think it, but you give more credence to one of them."

Madeline finished her sandwich and reached for some fruit. Hunger was as good an excuse as any to avoid answering Jode. But she couldn't delay forever. "Yes, I think Amberbirch is right. I think it is Springheart. Remember I didn't trust him at the beginning, and she said he'd vowed to destroy the elves."

Jode turned to her. "I'm surprised. You have known him much longer than you've known Amberbirch. Willowvine said it was Amberbirch, and yet you distrust Springheart."

She knew that Jode was right, but something made her believe Amberbirch. "It might not be a problem anyway. Willowvine didn't see that someone was going to sabotage us. She saw that they are seeking vengeance. I haven't asked her if it will be a problem for us. I don't think she knows more than emotional state, and I can't spend time worrying. I need you to think about how to deal with it if something happens. I have to focus on sealing the gate."

Jode didn't answer her. He tucked her into the blankets and cleared the dishes to the side. Then he slipped in beside her on the bed. "I will always watch for danger when it comes to you." He placed his hand on her belly. "I will always protect our children. You need not worry that someone will be able to destroy what you have worked so hard for."

She snuggled into his arms. "I know you'll be there. You are the only one I can trust." She felt the effects of the food and her exhaustion pull her into sleep. "Tomorrow we'll find the answer and then everything will be fine." She closed her eyes, and slipped into sleep, feeling loved and secure.

26

When she woke, Madeline saw that it was full dark outside – still night. They couldn't leave yet, but she knew that there was no chance to fall back asleep because Jode had left at some point in the last few hours, and his presence calmed her enough to rest. She untangled herself from the blanket, dressed, and went looking for him. Her feeling that she could put aside the problem of Willowvine's vision was not sitting well with her now that she was rested.

As she walked through the library in search of her husband, she felt alone. The library was silent in the way of buildings that were deserted. Knowing that the feeling couldn't be real, didn't make it any less disconcerting. She slowed her pace. What if they had all deserted her? How would she proceed? There was no doubt in her mind that she would continue the attempt to seal the well, but could she do it alone?

Would being alone be safer? Madeline shook off the feeling of dread the idea brought. No, she needed everyone around her, no matter their motivation. Jode was right; she'd known Springheart too long to think he'd destroy their hope. He could have managed that more easily by simply not finding her.

She must have been more tired than she'd thought to believe that anyone would want to destroy the world. The child must be wrong, or, if not wrong, mistaken. The only danger they faced, other than the gate itself, was this Scree. She wanted to know more about him. Perhaps if Willowvine could use her talent to get information on him, they would be better off.

As she neared the front entrance, Madeline heard voices. The presence of others seemed to warm the building. She followed the sound to see Amberbirch and Springheart sitting around a fire, glasses of wine in hand. Madeline wondered how the woman could have said those things about him, and then sit there so comfortably.

"Madeline, it is good to see you," Springheart said. "Are you looking for Jode?"

She watched Amberbirch turn to face her. The woman radiated kindness and sympathy. "He is checking the wagon and horses. Apparently, you have had problems with parts breaking before."

On the pass they'd been forced to use to reach the Choi, Madeline remembered the fear and noise of the wagon breaking free. "Are you going to get any sleep before we leave?"

Springheart placed his glass on the table. "We were going to retire soon. Shall I walk with you to Jode?"

"Yes, allow him to escort you," Amberbirch said. "The child says the Scree is approaching us. We would not want him to find you." She said goodnight and left them together.

SPRINGHEART WALKED Madeline toward the clearing where they had left the wagon, his thoughts occupied with too many concerns. How Willowvine would fare in this group. Was Willowvine's gang waiting? Was the Scree closer than they feared? "Tomorrow will be a day of good fortune," he said into the silence.

P. A. WILSON

Madeline stopped and turned; her face closed to him. She seemed to be watching him, looking for something. "I hope so," she said, and then started walking away.

"Madeline, is something wrong? Did I upset you with my message from Willowvine?" He moved more quickly to avoid losing her as they passed into the trees. "I thought it was—"

She held up a hand to stop him from speaking. "You did the right thing. I just don't like the implications. You think that Amberbirch is out to sabotage us, and I don't."

He didn't want to argue. Without proof, there was no use in creating bad feelings before they set out on the last stages of their task. "Then we will let things happen as they happen."

She looked at him again and then came to a stop. "When you found out that your father was dead, and you would have to leave the elves, what happened?"

Why was she asking about his past? "I was angry. I was a child. I lashed out. I said I would make them regret letting me go. The words of a child."

He watched as Madeline gathered her reaction to his words. How had she known?

"I want to believe that you…" she said.

"That I what? That I came to you with this information to hide my own motives? That I lowered myself into the well while I wanted to destroy this world?" He felt that same anger from his childhood rising. Something he had spent his whole life trying to master. He had let her make him feel as though he was part of a family, and it was clear that he wasn't. "I will leave if that makes you feel more safe."

Madeline didn't answer right away. Springheart knew that her words would hurt, whatever they were. If it wasn't for the danger of leaving her here without his protection, he would depart now. "Let us find Jode before he leaves the clearing."

"No, he can wait a little longer," she said. "Tell me what made

150

you change. What soothed that child? It must have been devastating to lose a parent, and then a people."

Her question surprised Springheart. Was she willing to believe he had overcome his past? "Life. I have lived long enough to know that there are ways to replace what the elves could not give me. I found friendships, and I learned to care for others."

She nodded and spoke quietly, "I know how that can happen."

"I do not know what I can do to assure you that I am faithful," he said.

"I don't know either," she answered. "I know that Jode believes in you. I know that you've been helpful, I know that, until Willowvine saw what she saw, I would never have though ill of you. Perhaps she has brought this on us. Perhaps it's all part of the puzzle. The gate is somehow twisting our minds."

"I do not think she was lying," he said. It was something he was sure of in his bones. "I also do not think she was mistaken."

Madeline closed her eyes and took a deep breath. "I don't either. It was all coming together so well." She took his arm. "Let's pretend it didn't happen."

He thought it wasn't wise to ignore the warning, but he would stay alert and so would Jode. That would have to be enough. "You have packed most of the library," he said.

"Yes. I don't know if there's anything there that will help," she admitted.

Springheart was glad to hear the shadow of doubt missing from her voice. Perhaps when her mentor arrived, he would help, and they would be done with this mess.

---

27

*T*he next morning as the sun rose, Madeline rode the wagon, reading on the short journey to the gate, making last minute notes and reviewing well-read pages of the books. Since Amberbirch had changed the spell on the paper, Madeline was convinced that there would be new meaning in the words she'd scoured before. There hadn't been any, and her confidence was fading with the lack of success. Even if there was nothing, she had to fill her time. As a lawyer, she'd always found the answers she needed in precedent. There was no reason the answer here would be found outside the books.

When the wagon arrived in the small clearing, Madeline left the others to set up and took Willowvine with her to the circle. She explained what they knew about the message, how the Scree had moved the stones, and what Springheart had found inside the well.

"What do you want me to do, Madeline," the girl asked. "I only see stones, and a hole in the center of the bowl."

Madeline had no illusions that Willowvine would find the answer, but she wanted the girl to have the same information as they all had. "Would you be able to use your magic to uncover any specific dangers?"

Willowvine pointed to the well. "That's the most apparent one," she said, and then laughed at Madeline's frustration. "It's very strong. I can feel the hatred. It's like a living being."

"A living being? I don't feel it that way. What else do you feel?"

Sitting, Willowvine patted the stone beside her. "I'll see what I can find. If I am in too long, you know what to do, right?"

Madeline nodded. She wouldn't let Willowvine drain her energy the way she'd done before. Springheart would never have let her get so weak if he'd known. She watched as the girl closed her eyes and relaxed into a trance. Keeping her focus firmly on the color of the girl's skin and the depth of her breathing, Madeline waited.

It was only a few minutes before Willowvine gasped and broke out of her trance. "The Scree is here." She pointed to a hill across the stone circle from where they sat.

Madeline called Jode and the others to join them as she waited for sight of the Scree who was possibly, no probably, going to attack. The men arrived with swords ready.

"Wait for him," Willowvine said. "He does not mean harm."

Jode stood in front of Madeline and the child. "Scree may not see killing us as harm. But we will not attack before it is necessary."

When the Scree crested the small hill, Madeline saw only a tall figure in gray robes. He walked slowly toward them, hands held out to the side, palms facing them. He was unarmed as far as she could see.

"Stop there," Jode called.

The Scree did as he was ordered. They stood facing each other for a long moment before Madeline spoke, "What do you want?"

He lifted the hood away from his face and she could see how

old he was. The oldest Scree she'd seen so far was the woman who worked for the ambassador in The City. Scree didn't live long lives as rule because of their warlike nature. This one looked older than the woman. His hair was long and braided, but thin and white. His skin was wrinkled and damaged from the sun. His eyes were the only feature that didn't look ancient; green and full of life.

"You are The Chosen," he said. "I have come to help you."

The three men moved closer, forming a wall between the Scree and Madeline. "What kind of help can a Scree give?"

Their visitor didn't react to the implied insult, another difference from all the other Scree Madeline had met. "It would be easier to tell my story if we were closer."

"Yes, and it would be easier for you to throw chalk and kill us if you were closer," Jode said before turning to Madeline. "Go back to the wagon and let the guards protect you while we deal with this," he ordered.

It was so unusual for Jode to order her to do anything that Madeline almost obeyed. But she sent Willowvine back and stood her ground. "I need to know how you deal with it."

He seemed about to repeat his order.

"Jode, I need to know how he passes or fails your interrogation. I cannot go into this wondering if it should have been different. I promise I won't get in the way."

He glared at her for a moment longer and then said, "Stay behind us, and do not try to stop what we are going to do."

She nodded agreement and stood back. Because the Scree was on the hill, she could still see him while safely behind her protectors.

"What is your name, Scree?" Springheart called.

"I am called by many names among my people, the old one, the wise one, but you may call me Rekart. And your names?"

Help still comes in the form of arrogance, Madeline thought. No matter how different this Rekart was from other scree, that remained a constant.

Springheart named them but did not mention the others. Rekart seemed satisfied with the information even though he could see that there were more people in their party.

"What can I do to assure you that I am to be trusted, at least in this endeavor," he asked.

Regis turned to Jode and said, "I will go to search him for weapons and chalk. If there are none, we can at least listen to him."

"Do Scree have any other magic?" Madeline asked. She wished that her own magic would give her some clue, but there was no reaction.

Springheart answered, "No, but this is not a normal Scree. I suggest that Regis bind him so he cannot use his hands as we listen. And I suggest we bring him back to the others before we hear his story. More eyes to watch his movements will be worth the risk of placing him within our entire party."

"Yes, and Amberbirch or Willowvine may be able to discern the truth of his words," Madeline added.

They gave the conditions to Rekart. He agreed and stood with his arms apart to allow Regis' search. When his pockets had been emptied of their contents, there were no bags of chalk waiting to be used for spell casting, Regis bound the Scree's arms behind him and escorted Rekart to their camp.

"I think we will be safe to listen," Regis said. "If we do not like what he has to say, we will also be in a position to deal with it."

Madeline walked up to Rekart and looked into his eyes. "Do you plan to harm us?"

He held her gaze. "I will not harm anyone who is trying to seal that gate. I will do more than harm to anyone who acts to prevent that from happening."

"Then let us hear your story," she said.

28

*W*hen they arrived at the wagon, the three guards were waiting for them. Madeline told them to relax and asked Amberbirch to join the party. Before they allowed Rekart to tell his story, she took Willowvine aside.

In the few minutes between meeting Rekart and returning to the wagon, Madeline had come up with a plan. "Do you think you could tell if he is lying?" she asked.

Willowvine smiled at her. "Yes, I did it all the time for my gang. It was important that we knew our contacts were reliable. I can tell his intentions," she said. "That might not be consistent with his actions."

"That's good enough. If his intentions are to tell us the truth, he'll do it. If his facts are wrong… well, he's in the same boat as we are," Madeline said, hope rising in her that this would be progress rather than a new obstacle. "What do we need to do?"

Willowvine looked to where the others waited. "I need to sit across from him. It doesn't take much energy to read him. So as long as he doesn't take hours to tell his story, I should be fine."

"If he is lying, you need to tell me," Madeline said. "Don't worry about interrupting, or politeness, just say what you think."

"I may need to ask questions," Willowvine said. "I sometimes feel like there is more than they are saying. I need to know if it's a lie or just something else."

Madeline told Willowvine to ask whatever she needed, but it would be good to allow Rekart to tell his story without guidance. They joined the others and Madeline told Rekart to start.

He nodded and looked around the circle. He seemed to be assessing the value of each of the members of the team. Madeline noticed him stop when he looked at Amberbirch. A frown crossed his face briefly, but then he moved on. When he was finished, Rekart told his story to Madeline, ignoring everyone else.

"You know the Scree as violent people. I am sure that you expect me to attack given a chance. I am not as these new Scree. I am from a place where we kept purity in our spirits. A place few know of and none remember but the ten who live there." He paused and licked his lips. Madeline instructed a guard to feed Rekart some water.

"Thank you, Chosen One," he said. "In this place, my brothers and I keep the old ways as much as we can."

"We know of the old ways of the Scree," Amberbirch said. "You kill. You take. You attack."

Madeline was already tired of his dancing around. Knowing that Amberbirch's words wouldn't help move the story along, she didn't acknowledge the accusation. "What are the old ways?" She refrained from asking if they involved sacrifice or torture.

"Impatience is understandable at this juncture," he said unmoved by her words. "The Scree were not so violent in our own world. When we were taken from there, we were merchants, and philosophers, and teachers. We had warriors yes, but all people have that. We were many tribes and there were wars, but that was not our only life. We honored wisdom as well as warfare."

157

Madeline looked at Willowvine, the girl hadn't moved from her position, her eyes were closed, her face calm.

"So, you remember the time you came here," Madeline asked.

"Yes. We keep records and pass the memory along the generations." He paused as if to re-gather his place in the story. "Our lives have changed for the worst since we came to this world. The war that met us, gave too much power to the warriors. After the battles, the only way for us to survive seemed to be allowing the warriors to take control."

"That happened very quickly," Amberbirch said bitterly. "Many elves were lost to the battle."

"A violent wind pulled us from our homes. We lived on one continent close together because our world was mostly water and ice. The wind came, and we found ourselves forced through the darkness to a strange land. One where there were only armed warriors who charged us with swords and rained arrows among us as we recovered. What would you have had us do?"

"You blame us for your behavior all these years?" Amberbirch asked. "Even after the battle, you remained violent and untrustworthy."

"Let him tell the story before we judge him," Madeline said. She was tired of waiting for something that would help them. This history of the Scree would have been interesting at a different time, but they didn't have the luxury for small talk. "How does this relate to our purpose?"

"I am getting to that," Rekart said. "There were twelve families who refused to join the new order. We took ourselves to one of the islands and kept the record of what we used to be. We gathered books from others, and learned that there was a way to seal the gate between worlds. I am here to help."

Madeline couldn't stem the feeling of relief. Willowvine hadn't stopped him, so what he told them was the truth in his eyes. Help was welcome from any corner of this world. If the elves had asked for help, maybe the well would have been closed before now.

"How can you help," Jode asked.

"There were two messages. The one that I believe you have already deciphered, and one that I have deciphered. Between these two is the method of sealing the gate."

Willowvine came out of her trance when that statement was made. "It is all the truth."

Madeline rubbed at the burning itch that had flushed her skin; not only was it true, it was vital. It made her wonder what was missing from the information she had at hand. If Rekart had not appeared, would they have made some mistake because they didn't know some detail? "We have the messages. There are two ways to seal the gate," she said as she cut the bonds they'd placed on him. "One will seal for a thousand years and will require less of a sacrifice, the other will seal it permanently."

Rekart rubbed his hands bringing the circulation back. "Yes, one will require a sacrifice from you, the other a sacrifice of someone."

"How do you know that?" Madeline asked, suddenly suspicious.

"My message is the same."

The relief she'd felt disappeared. "If yours is the same, how can you help?"

Before Rekart could answer, Amberbirch interjected, "He cannot. The Scree cannot be trusted. The girl said he spoke the truth, but how do we know that his truth is the same as ours?"

"We don't, but neither do I know your truth is the same as mine, or Springheart's. And you know we are all different." Madeline didn't want to share their recent suspicions with Rekart. She turned to the Scree. "If your message is the same, how can you help?"

"I have more than that in my message," he said. "I know what we need to do to enact the ceremony that will close the gate, and I may have knowledge about the sacrifices that you may choose."

29

_M_adeline's heart leapt at the hope Rekart held out. She was so used to fearing Scree, and fighting them, and killing too many of them, to feel comfortable trusting one. She did trust Willowvine's magic, at least enough for this. "Can we just get it over with right now?"

Rekart's smile was an uncomfortable reminder of the pleasure Sayer Goddard had expressed when he thought he had won the blood feud with Arabela. Madeline pushed the image away and waited, praying that the answer would be yes.

"I think it is best that we go to the well to discuss this. There are some items we need to gather, but they are not uncommon. The challenge is the date of the ceremony. I believe we need to be together to find that answer." He struggled to his feet, and Madeline was reminded again of his age. "I do know that there is a date, but I do not know when it is. Let us hope we will discover that the ceremony can be completed within the next few days at most." He looked at the other members of their party. "I do not think I will be welcome here for much longer."

Madeline allowed Jode to pull her into a standing position. "We have had bad experiences at the well." She told Rekart how the wind and dust attacked them when they approached. "I don't want to be forced into the well, so we will need to be tethered."

Rekart agreed to be bound and so the two of them approached the well safely attached at the other end of the ropes to two of the guards. "Was there any warning of the attack?" he asked.

Madeline tried to remember if there had been anything that would serve as a warning. In her mind, the wind had been sudden, but the force grew rather than being there at the onset. The dust had always come after the wind reached full force. "We need to be vigilant for any change in the breeze."

Standing on the last ring of stones next to a Scree was the most disturbing feeling. Madeline was able to sense the difference between the two threats. The well was real, hatred radiated from the darkness like a pulse on her skin, as though she was living within the heart of another being. The Scree threat was pale in comparison, and in her own mind rather than his physical presence.

"So, what should we be looking for," she asked. "We've deciphered every message we could find and there was no specific date." She was worn out from feeling they'd made progress only to have the hope dashed as yet another hurdle appeared.

Rekart bent to touch the inside of the well, just the surface of the stones ringing the entrance. The rope became taut as the two guards on the end took up the slack. He was able to pass his hand across the stone, but he would not fall in.

"There will be a sign," he said. "Feel here." He took her hand and placed it against the carved words.

Madeline concentrated, pushing away the suffocating feeling of evil that rose from the depths of the gate. "There's a channel. How is that going to help us?"

"Feel how it circles around the opening, and how there are vertical notches." He waited for her to confirm his findings. "I think this is a sun calendar. If we were to construct a rim with projecting posts, it would fit inside."

"So, it throws a shadow onto a specific stone?" Madeline asked. "How will we know that the shadow hits the right stone?"

Rekart rose and helped Madeline to stand. "Sun calendars are very specific in design. Each is identical in height and number of posts and diameter. If we can find one, it will fit. If we need to construct one, it will take only a few hours."

Madeline wiped the dust from her hands. "And how will we know what date to do the ceremony?"

Rekart looked around him. "It is not a date as much as a count down. I believe that the original builders meant the shadow from the sun calendar to start touching the stones at the first one and then each day at mid-day it will touch a new stone. There must be a hundred days here," he said. "A hundred days would have given ample time to bring an army to defend against the people drawn here."

"How on earth would that be forgotten or lost?" Madeline felt her anger growing at the foolishness of the creators of the circle. Yes, she knew that the gate could only be sealed at the right time, but how would they know to be ready for the battle?

"There are probably other signs that the well is opening," he said. "Is no one making preparations in case you fail?"

"Yes, there is an army coming. This time it's not just the elves," Madeline said. "There's something more than the countdown to this." She closed her eyes to shut out distractions. The elves knew that the gate was opening, and yet Amberbirch had not known about the calendar. The answer clicked into her mind as though someone had spoken. "It's a countdown for me. If I don't seal the well within the time set by the stones, the ceremony won't work."

"Then let us hope that the shadow does not appear on the last stone," Rekart said. "I am certain it has already passed the first one."

Madeline turned to walk back to the wagon. "We can go to

the library and find a calendar. Tomorrow, we'll test your theory. If we have no time, we will need to act."

His response was cut off by a hissing from the well. The wind had not increased. Madeline felt no threat of being pulled into the hole, so she turned to see what was causing the noise. Nothing rose from the well. She stepped to the limit of her rope. It allowed her to stand at the edge of the well after she gave a slight tug to get more slack.

There was a dim glow of light shining at her. "I hope that's not the opening," she said to Rekart who had joined her.

"No, the wind is the passage." He leaned further over.

"Do not interfere with my work." The words roared at them. Madeline rocked back from the edge of the well. The voice continued, "Attempt my death at your peril, Chosen One. I will not die easily."

She waited, ears ringing, for more.

"Silence will not help you. I have allies and you will fail. I will feed again, and you will be the first morsel."

She felt the wind start to rise and pulled at Rekart's arm. "Run!" She turned and sprinted toward the edge of the stones.

he ropes that were supposed to save them, tripped Madeline as they passed out of the main force of the wind. Rekart caught her before she landed on the stones. "It would not do for you to be injured just before we complete our quest," he said, lifting her off her feet and carrying her the last few steps to where everyone waited.

Jode ran to take her from the Scree's hands. "Are you hurt?" he asked as he placed her on her feet and ran his hands along her arms. "What happened out there?"

Madeline wiggled out of his embrace, assuring him that she was perfectly fine. "There was a voice," she gasped. "There is something alive in the well."

Rekart related the message they'd received. "I think it would be best to return to your library. If this creature has woken enough to speak, I am not certain that it cannot hear us. We must decide what to do with this knowledge."

Jode nodded to the Scree and helped Madeline to the wagon. "Rekart can ride with you," he said. He leaned close to add in whisper, "Do not trust him so easily. He is a Scree, no matter what he tells us about being a scholar."

Madeline glanced at Rekart. "I know, but you need to hear what we found."

"He can take my horse," Amberbirch insisted. "I would feel better if he was where you can see his every move. Not so close to Madeline where he can do harm." She climbed onto the seat beside Madeline, as though everyone had agreed. "We will talk about this new development as we ride."

Madeline didn't want to talk about it, at least until everyone was together. "I don't think it will change what we do," she said. "Sealing the well is the goal. If that means we have to kill this thing, I won't apologize for it."

Amberbirch didn't reply. Madeline watched the woman as she took in the declaration. Was she thinking of a way to stop them? Was there something she knew about this entity? Madeline could tell that there was something coming, but she was happy to wait, thinking it couldn't be good. As helpful as Amberbirch had been, she was becoming more bitter the closer they were getting. At that thought, she felt a wave of pity for Amberbirch. Her words had been sharper than she intended. "When we were there, at the well, Rekart did find something." It couldn't hurt to discuss the calendar, she thought. She told Amberbirch what they had found inside. "Is there one at the library?"

"It is interesting that the Scree was the one to see this," she replied. "Springheart was inside the well. Why would he have not seen this channel?"

Madeline tried not to react to the accusation. She'd thought they were past this pointing of fingers. "Perhaps it wasn't there at the time. The stones have changed, since we uncovered The Stone of Lilyriver. Perhaps the channel was hidden. And you remember he almost fell into the depths. Perhaps he had no time to see more than the words."

Amberbirch checked for the riders. Madeline saw that Springheart was in the rear of their company. Rekart rode between the guards in front of Springheart, Regis in front of him.

If Rekart was hoping to flee, he would not be able to get his horse more than two steps before someone would be in the way. Jode rode beside them, Willowvine behind him on the saddle. The girl was watching Amberbirch. Madeline made a mental note to ask her why when they were alone.

Apparently deciding she was safe to speak, Amberbirch continued, "You are a loyal friend to him. It is good that one of our orphans has found someone like you. As to how he missed the sun calendar bracket, we can ask him when we return. I would like to know more about this Rekart as well. I have never heard of a scholarly Scree," Amberbirch said, clearly unwilling to give up her need to undermine Springheart unless she could transfer it to someone else.

"And the sun calendar?" Madeline reminded her.

"There is one in the library. It is old and should be tended before we try to use it. I will have one of the servants oil the wood and ensure nothing is broken."

Madeline was silent for the rest of the short ride. Amberbirch was deep in her own thoughts, so it was a peaceful journey. The sun was still warm as it dropped to the horizon, but the nights were getting cold. Winter would be on them soon. It was a long journey back to her home, and if they stayed too late, she worried that they would be stuck in the elven lands until spring. And the twins would be born here not in her home as she'd hoped.

As they rode into the small courtyard, Madeline remembered that Blu would arrive tomorrow. "Perhaps Regis can find out how far Blu is from us. I think we need his advice more than ever." She was not going to delay their return with the calendar for long. She had this growing unease that the shadow was going to land on the final stone tomorrow.

"You must be looking forward to seeing your other friends as well," Amberbirch said. "They are returning with the priest? It will be good for you to have people you can truly trust."

Madeline smiled. Perhaps they would be done by tomorrow

night. Then she could relax and enjoy the company of her friends. Then they could start living the future she really wanted. She climbed down from the wagon and followed the others into the library.

MADELINE SEARCHED OUT REGIS. He was sitting in the garden, eyes closed and apparently enjoying the rest.

She approached quietly. If he was sleeping, she would leave him to his rest and ask later.

"Yes, Madeline?" he asked opening his eyes.

"How did you know I was here?" She had been careful to make no noise.

He glanced at her belly. "I hear children. When you are near, I hear laughter."

She placed her hand on the roundness, feeling a gentle kick from inside. They were content right now. "You hear them? Should I?" A tingle of jealousy ran through her.

"I don't know," he said. "I thought it was because they took my magic, but they took yours too. If you do not hear their joy, perhaps there is another reason."

"When we are done with the gate, we can find out." Madeline wasn't concerned; the kids were fine, she told herself. The twins had shown an independent streak almost from conception.

She asked Regis if he could find Blu. "They should be close, right?" The ache to see her friends again was stronger since Amberbirch mentioned it.

He closed his eyes and Madeline waited for him to complete the search. After a few minutes, Regis returned to the present. "They will arrive tomorrow morning. Would you like me to give them a message?"

"No. I'd like to scry him. Can you give me something to focus on?" Bringing Blu up to date before he arrived was a good idea. It would save time. Madeline wanted to be the one who did that if possible.

"What do you need?"

She realized Regis never needed anything to focus on when he contacted people. She'd assumed it was a form of scrying, but it wasn't. It was another interesting facet of magic. "Anything I can use for a focus. I usually know where the person is when I scry, so I use a room, or a landmark. If you can give me a description of the wagon they travel in, that should be enough."

Regis closed his eyes again, this time it only took a few seconds for him to answer, "The only thing I can see is Blu's cloak, the wagon is nondescript."

She thanked him and said reluctantly, "I'll wait. What do you think of the events of today?" She had not intended to ask, but Madeline realized that she needed a point of view to counter Amberbirch's suspicions.

"Did you ever think you would be asking my advice after what I did to Tadric?" He laughed, but the sound was a little weak, as though he was trying to hide his emotions.

Madeline guessed that Regis was afraid that he hadn't been forgiven. It was unlikely that feeling would go away until he was in Arabela's house. The forgiveness he needed was hers, and his own. "You've proven to be a good friend, and not only to me."

That seemed to give him some comfort. "The day was eventful. I think the appearance of a learned Scree was enough of a surprise. Then we received an answer to some of our questions. I am prepared to be optimistic, but a big part of me worries that Rekart's appearance was very convenient."

So, it wasn't just her. Rekart's presence was disconcerting to say the least. Her instinct was to attack, or run. But he hadn't threatened anyone. He had been calm and informative. She didn't need Willowvine to tell her that he was truthful, but something deep inside was keeping her suspicion alive. "I guess we'll find out sooner rather than later. What about the fact that Springheart hadn't seen the calendar channel?" She hated to give life to those suspicions, but she needed to hear his answer so she could determine whether or not she should give credence to Amberbirch.

"I trust Springheart," Regis said. "If the channel was there, he missed seeing it for a good reason. Perhaps the perspective of the light was wrong." Regis looked into Madeline's eyes. "He would not choose to destroy his people by omission. If he were going to do that, he would make it more personal. And he could have simply not found you. Without you, there would be no hope to avoid a bloody and devastating battle."

As Regis spoke, Madeline felt the truth resonate. "I hadn't thought of that." Since he was in an advising mood, she continued, "And Rekart? How do you think we'll know to trust him?"

Regis stood and held out his hand to assist Madeline. "Willowvine does not see anything in his aura to worry about."

"She's a child. Would she know what we should worry about?" Madeline shivered; the nights were becoming chilly. "I want to believe he's an ally, but as you said, it seems to be too convenient."

Regis led her to the kitchen. "Do not measure elven maturity against human. She may be young, but Willowvine has not been a child as we think of them for a long time. As for Rekart, I hope that is because we have become too used to the complexity we see around us. Perhaps Blu can help when he arrives. But Madeline, sometimes convenience is not to be suspected. It is just the universe aligning for you."

31

---

*A*fter warming up in the kitchen, Madeline gathered everyone in the room where she'd been studying for months, where The Stone of Lilyriver had almost torn them apart. Now she was hoping they would get the last of the information they needed. Tomorrow as soon as Blu arrived, they were going back to the gate, they'd have their reunion there while she sealed it.

When everyone was arranged in the room, wine, or caf, in hand, she asked Rekart to explain his information. "Start with what you know about the ceremony." She wasn't willing to hear about the sacrifice yet; she knew she wouldn't like the answer.

He leaned forward and started talking, "Before I tell you about the ceremony, let me summarize what I think we both know."

Madeline wanted to get to the meat of the story. "Can we just go back to that when you've told us the ceremony?"

"You are impatient," Rekart said. "If you will allow me to tell this at my pace, it will be better. I am worried that we will miss some important facet of our plan."

She nodded for him to continue. Hoping that he would not turn it into a lecture, she sat back.

"I only know this about your side of the prophecy," he continued. "You will have two choices, one that will seal the gate for a thousand years, the other will seal it permanently. You think that the permanent solution will cost the life of one of your friends."

Madeline nodded.

"If you need it, I will give my life to seal the gate," Springheart said.

"Let us not be too quick to offer our lives," Rekart said holding up his hand to stop other interruptions.

"We have avoided this conversation for too long," Jode said. "I would be willing to go into that hole, if it meant the future of my children."

"No," Madeline said. "I don't want to talk about anyone going in that well. We don't know it's required. Let's hear what Rekart has to say."

He waited for them all to relax and then continued, "There are two ceremonies. If you choose to only seal the gate for one thousand years, we will conduct a simple ceremony in which you cast the thing you are willing to sacrifice into the well and it is done." He paused but no one had any questions. "I do not know what this creature will do during the ceremony. It is the first time I have heard of such a thing."

Madeline thought it was too easy. "So, I just decide on something I don't want any longer and toss it in?"

"It must be something of great value," Rekart said. "You will not be able to complete the spell with a jewel or other trinket."

Regis leaned forward. "I think the entity will fight back. If it controls the wind, will you be able to toss something in?"

Madeline waved away the concern. "We'll find a way to allow me to stay there until we are done. What about the other choice?" Even if she didn't want to sacrifice anyone, she needed to know. A permanent solution would be the best one. She hoped that the cost was something she could live with. She feared that it would need to be her. If she wasn't pregnant, she would do it without thought, but the children deserved a chance to live.

Rekart looked at his hands, his reluctance plain in his actions. "It will be a death. It will have to be a death that is not voluntary." He looked up. "I am sorry to have to say that. If I could, I would volunteer. I have lived all my life in history. I would not flinch at ending it in building a future."

"I won't talk about it now. What is that ceremony?" Madeline walked to the window. It was full night. The stars bright with frost. "Just tell us and we can move on. Maybe sleep before we have to go back."

"There will need to be a battle. Blood must be spilled on this side of the gate; it is how the gate is always closed. But if the transfer of beings has been completed first, the gate will reopen." He took a sip from his glass and waited.

"If it is just a matter of blood being spilled, we can still volunteer," Springheart said.

Before Rekart could answer, Amberbirch spoke for the first time. "How do you know this in such detail? We have nothing so clear in our message. How can we trust that this information is real?"

"He is not lying," Willowvine said.

"Yes, child, but that may simply mean that he believes what he says, not that what he says is the truth." Amberbirch smiled at the girl. It seemed kind, but Madeline saw the condescension in her manner.

Willowvine closed her mouth as though biting back a response.

"Let him answer," Madeline said. The arguing was getting on her nerves. Between people volunteering to die, and Amberbirch challenging the only person with information, she was losing her patience.

"I do not know why your message was vague. I followed the

173

clues and each step was precisely laid out. Why is your message so unclear?"

Madeline figured that he was feeling the same frustration as she was. "It was probably my fault," she said. Shaking her head at the protestations, she continued, "I don't read even modern elvish. I'm sure if I knew more, I could have found the answers. It doesn't matter, we have the answers now." Something made her keep the discovery of the plain messages to herself.

"Yes, and we are tired. Is there anything we can do to prepare tonight?" Jode asked. "If there is only debate over how we arrived at this knowledge, I will take my wife to bed. If we are to do battle in the next few days, we will all benefit from rest."

No one tried to argue with him. Madeline didn't know if she would sleep, but she knew that resting was better than this. "Blu will be here tomorrow. When he arrives, we'll take the calendar to the well and see how much time we have."

Regis stood and offered his room to Rekart. "I have an idea for harnesses. If the wind is sent again, we need to hold our ground. Ropes won't help. I'll sleep in the kitchen when I'm done." He escorted the Scree from the room.

As they were leaving, one of the servants approached. "Two scouts have arrived. An elf and a human. The army is only a day behind."

Jode told the servant to house the scouts in the kitchen. "Madeline, I will talk to them. You must rest."

"If the army is only a day behind, we know what the calendar will show," she said. "We are too late."

He folded her in an embrace, holding her close for a long moment. "We do not know that. An army does not arrive at a battle at the last minute. I have faith that there will be time for you to do what is necessary. This army will go home unscathed."

Jode left her in the hall, after ensuring that she would go to their room and sleep, or at least try to. Madeline watched him go. He always had the energy to do what needed to be done. She was getting more tired by the minute. Tonight, she knew she would sleep no matter what her nerves felt about tomorrow. She started up the stairs thinking about her bed.

"Madeline, a moment, please," Amberbirch said.

Madeline stopped and turned to face the elven woman. "Can it wait until morning? I need to rest so I will have the energy for the gate."

Amberbirch joined Madeline on the stairs. "It will only take moment, and we can talk on the way to your room."

She didn't have the energy to argue, so Madeline allowed Amberbirch to take her arm and lead her toward the living quarters.

"I wanted to talk to you in private. Too many people have joined us in the last few days and I worry that we are losing our focus," Amberbirch said.

Madeline heard the bitterness in the woman's tone. Amberbirch had always been the leader, the one to guide their research, to find the clues. She was right, since Willowvine had joined them, everyone else had taken that role. She was feeling left out. The least Madeline could do was hear what she wanted to say. "I think we are all still very much focused on sealing the gate."

"Are you certain that this new information is the truth? We have no reason to believe the child." Amberbirch patted her hand. "I know that you like her. You have a fondness for orphans it seems, first Springheart, now this bandit child. But she has had little experience of the world."

Far from having a fondness for orphans, the old Madeline would have simply called social services, and figured she was doing the right thing. "Willowvine was able to tell us that Rekart was coming."

Amberbirch patted her hand again. "Yes, that was helpful. It is odd that she didn't notice the army."

"Yes, it is," Madeline said, wondering why she hadn't thought of that. "But we didn't ask her to reach out for them."

"They would have been close when she looked for, and found, this feeling of vengeance," Amberbirch said. "An army does not move that quickly."

"They aren't a threat to us," Madeline said. "She was looking for threats. Is there anything else? This is my room."

She hoped Amberbirch would let the subject drop. Madeline didn't need to start second guessing what they already knew. The elven woman cocked her head, assessing Madeline. "Let me come in and help you go to sleep. I have some herbs here." She drew a bag out of the pocket in her robe.

Madeline started to say no but changed her mind. She couldn't risk not sleeping tonight. "Will you need to make a tea?"

Amberbirch opened the door to Madeline's room. "No. In your condition, it would not be wise to drink something like this. I'll burn them in the candle flame. The fumes will be sufficient."

They entered the small room. It contained a bed and a table with a lit candle on it. There was one tiny window high on the wall. It didn't provide much light even at midday. Madeline invited Amberbirch to sit on the bed, since there were no chairs. "I'm grateful for your help," she said.

Shaking the contents of the bag into the bowl of a silver spoon, Amberbirch muttered a few words over them. "It has been my honor. I am sorry to be so suspicious of your new friends. I should trust your instincts."

Madeline watched as pale smoke rose from the spoon that the elven woman was holding over the candle. It smelled sweet and clean in the room, and she felt her body relax from the tension that had been holding it taut since the voice within the well first spoke.

Amberbirch smiled and waved the smoke toward Madeline. "I worry because this is the future of the whole world. I am here to help you, Madeline. I do not know what others are here to do."

"You are right to be concerned. I promise I won't be foolish. Willowvine is just a child, and I don't see how she can harm us. I think Rekart is an ally, but," she yawned in mid-sentence. "But I will keep your words in mind."

"That is all I ask," Amberbirch said as she stood. "Now lay down and let the herbs do their work."

Madeline's eyes closed on their own. She felt the covers being tucked around her, and then heard the sound of the door closing.

32

*T*he next morning, Madeline felt refreshed, if not completely rested. The herbs had worked. She remembered rousing when Jode climbed into bed, but then falling immediately back to sleep.

As she reached the main floor, the sound of voices greeted her. Voices she hadn't heard in a long time. Madeline ran toward the sound. They were in the kitchen. Simon, Blu, and the others. She ran to give Simon a hug and then turned to Blu. They didn't usually hug, she hesitated, but then he held out his arms in welcome.

"Madeline, it is good to see you again," he said. "You look healthy."

"Blu, I missed you so much. When did you arrive?" He motioned for her to sit beside him.

"We have been here for long enough to learn everything you have discovered. To meet your extraordinary companions, and to eat." His voice relaxed her fears. "I understand we are to leave again soon for this gate. To assess how much time we have until the moment of fate."

"As soon as there is enough light to travel," Madeline said. "We have time to eat, and talk."

Amberbirch cleared the room of everyone until only the three of them were sitting at the table. "We have given the facts, but there is always more to discuss." She poured caf for Madeline. "You must eat while you talk. We have only an hour at the most."

Blu looked at Amberbirch. Madeline saw he was assessing the woman. When he spoke, it was to Madeline, "Is this gate so far away that we need to leave now to arrive when the sun is high?" When Madeline assured him that it was only an hour away at most, he continued, "If the calendar is to indicate the days until the gate opens, then we do not need to be there immediately."

Madeline started to answer, but Amberbirch interrupted, "We have preparations, and you will need to examine the area. Madeline hopes to seal the gate today."

Blu nodded. "I think that is a wise course." He leaned toward Amberbirch. "You have been a good friend and adviser, I think. Would you begrudge me a little time alone with my student?"

Madeline watched as a flash of annoyance crossed Amberbirch's face. She thought the woman was feeling jealous. "Please, Amberbirch. I have so much to talk to Blu about. You will be bored with the details. I'm sure the others need you to check that the calendar is properly protected."

It was clear that Amberbirch wanted to argue, but after looking at Blu and Madeline, she rose. "We will be waiting at the wagon for you."

When they were alone, Blu took Madeline's hands. "You are troubled."

The statement was simple, but it dug into Madeline's heart. All of the worries and suspicions overwhelmed her. Drawing a deep breath to hold the tears at bay, Madeline told Blu about what Willowvine had seen. "I can't stop suspecting everyone. One minute I am defending someone, the next I am watching for evidence of betrayal."

He gave her hands a squeeze. "I am sorry you have been left to do this alone. It is not surprising to me that you are confused. You are being asked to trust someone who looks like an old enemy. Only Jode is familiar to you. These others are all strangers."

She wiped away the tears that had fallen despite her attempt to control the emotions. "I trust Jode, but he doesn't really understand what I have to do. Only someone with magic can know."

"That is true," he said. Lifting her chin, he looked into her eyes. "It is also true that you find it hard to ask for help. Have you been leaning on your husband? Or have you been trying to protect him from whatever is to come?"

Madeline blushed at the accusation she felt in his words. Blu would never intend a rebuke; he had always been patient with her mistakes and lack of understanding. She placed her hand on her belly and nodded. "I can't protect these beyond giving them a place to grow. If I let Jode know what I really fear... No, I can't take the chance that he would stop me doing what needs to be done."

"He is a soldier," Blu said. "You think that he doesn't know the strength of the enemy, and that he thinks the army can do what is necessary."

Jode had never said anything like that to her, but Madeline knew that was exactly what he thought. "If it came to sacrificing his life, he wouldn't hesitate. I'm afraid that I will have to sacrifice mine. And that means these two will die with me. It is something I can't even think about seriously. I just tell myself that I'll do what is needed."

"So, that is the reason you are unwilling to discuss a permanent solution?" he asked. "You think that the sacrifice will be your life for that solution?"

She nodded. "A thousand years is a long time to find another way to deal with the gate."

He sighed and closed his eyes. Madeline was used to seeing

him react like that. He was searching his mind for an answer. She waited, no longer feeling the urgency to rush to the gate.

After a few moments, Blu opened his eyes. "Everything that I have been told leads me to the conclusion that you will not be required to sacrifice your life. The words you found were, the sacrifice that seals the gate for eternity will come from one without ties. You have ties."

"I have some," Madeline said. "We all have some ties. But I am a stranger here. Surely that has something to do with me being The Chosen."

"I cannot say what the answer is, but I have a strong feeling that I am right." He gave her hands another squeeze. "What would you sacrifice to seal the gate for a thousand years?"

Madeline had been asking herself that question from the moment they had translated the message. "It has to be something I can give now, so it won't be the babies."

Blu didn't react, he simply waited for her to continue. Madeline felt that same mixture of frustration and curiosity that accompanied her lessons. While it would be quicker for Blu to answer, he knew that she would feel the excitement of accomplishment, and remember the lesson, if he let her get to it by herself.

"It has to be something I value, and I don't really have anything here. And the voice didn't seem like it was interested in material things." She paused to gather herself before she could continue. "I think it might be Jode. He is what I value most." Her voice cracked with the fear she felt.

Blu wiped tears from her cheeks and patted her arm. "We will not know until the time comes. If the price is Sir Jode, you must decide if his death is worth such a temporary result."

33

hile Blu's words didn't exactly bring Madeline comfort, they did give her a sense of peace. It helped to put aside the sinking feeling that she was missing something important.

"So, what do we do?" Madeline knew that only a few minutes had passed since she'd realized there was no need to arrive at the gate so early, but she still didn't want to keep the others waiting. "I still think there is a best way to deal with this."

Blu settled into the cushions of the seat. It was a normal size, but he seemed lost in it. Age was shrinking him. Regardless of the physical aging, he was still healthy, eyes bright and mind sharp. "There is a spell. It will focus that power you have to predict the future of events."

Hope lit Madeline's heart. If she could foresee the future, then she'd get her answers. "Let's do it."

Blu gestured for her to get comfortable. "We will meet on the beach you use to focus your mind. When we are there, you can ask the fates to show you the choices. Sometimes that means you will be able to understand which choice is right."

Madeline knew it wouldn't just be a quick question and

answer session, but she felt disappointment anyway. "Okay, what do I need to tell you so you can be there?"

Blu held up a hand; a familiar request for patience. "There is something that you need to know before we do this." He waited until she nodded. "When we are there, I will see your true spirit. You will only see me as I am now."

When Madeline had seen the children, she'd seen human children. She assumed that they had only seen her. "Why?"

"We have different magic," he said taking her hands. "Are you sure you are willing to let me see your spirit?"

She nodded. Not worried because Blu had never thought her a perfect person and she had never been fool enough to think she was anything other than a mix of good and bad.

He continued, "Now relax and picture this beach. I will follow your lead."

Madeline went through her exercise of centering her thoughts on the sandy beach. The sound of the waves lulled her, the heat from the sun and sand was comforting, and the taste of salt in the air was a taste of homecoming. She opened her eyes to see the usual vision, this time Blu stood in front of her. As predicted, he looked the same as he did outside the vision, tiny, wrinkled, and wise. His expression didn't reflect what he saw, so Madeline felt somewhat relieved that she hadn't grown horns or burst into flames.

She asked him what the spell was, and Blu explained the type of question, and how to call the magic to her in this imaginary world.

Madeline kept a firm hold on Blu's hands as she spoke the question. She looked to the wide expanse of sand leading up to the tree line. "I request knowledge of the ceremony to seal the gate between worlds. One sacrifice of mine, one sacrifice from others."

They waited. Madeline tried to keep her focus on the sand, but Blu's intense stare that never moved from her face, was distracting.

That was, until the sand began to move.

It started with a faint shifting of a few grains and then accelerated until it seemed like an artist was painting a scene on the beach. Two furrows raced from her to separate places on the sand. One stopped and formed a circle. Within the circle, a whirlwind spun into two separate columns, and continued into the distance, stopping when it reached the line of grass. At the end, it started throwing sand in the air, not forming shapes, just a mass of sand, then the trees started to wave. Then a heart formed and dissolved, then another, then more until the whole line of sand between them and the trees was forming hearts that melted almost as soon as they were recognizable shapes.

It stopped and Madeline focused on the closer circle. It formed a tall column of whirling sand with a heart beating in the center. She thought there was a twin column just behind the first.

Looking back to the other path, Madeline saw the two columns shift into one, then a mist of fine sand buried the column.

Loss hollowed out her body. Madeline felt tears washing through the dust that filled the air from the images. Blu let go of her hands, and she found herself in the kitchen, face still wet from tears, but no trace of the violence of what they'd experienced. Exhaustion robbed Madeline of the strength to remain upright. She slumped. The world went gray, but she struggled to remain conscious.

"Eat this," Blu's voice broke through the fog. "I did not expect it to take so much out of you."

His hand under her chin, Blu raised Madeline's head. She opened her mouth to take the spoon of honey he offered. It provided her with enough energy to feed herself the porridge that he handed her next. A few mouthfuls were all she could manage before needing to talk about what they'd seen.

Fearful that his experience had been different, Madeline asked Blu what had happened.

"I saw what you saw, Madeline," he answered. "What do you think is the meaning of the two different paths?"

Feeling more energized from the food, and the fact that they had witnessed the same event, Madeline gathered her thoughts. "No matter what, I am going to lose something I love. If I choose one path, the one to permanently seal the gate, it feels like the loss is all mine. If I choose the other, I will lose less, but eventually everyone will die when the gate opens again."

Blu gestured for her to keep eating. "I think that may be close to the truth. But do not forget that you knew the choice to seal the gate for one thousand years would result in its opening again. The vision did not say that everyone would die, only that there would be many deaths. If you choose that solution, in one thousand years this world will be ready. It will not just be the elves. It will be all of Cartref."

As much as she wanted to believe that the violence in the future would not result in the death of everyone on this world, Madeline felt the deep certainty that she was right. "I can't take that chance."

Blu pushed the empty bowl to the center of table and took her hands. "Do not make your final decision until we know what you will have to sacrifice. The future is never certain. Even if you end this peril, there will be other threats to the lives of our descendants."

She drew her hands back and placed them on her stomach. Echoes of the pain of future generations flooded her, bringing the tears back. "Let's hope we will learn more when we arrive at the circle," she said, feeling no confidence that they would.

"Yes." Blu seemed willing to ignore her lie. "You must eat something more before we leave. And I must tell you what else I learned while we were on your wonderful beach."

He waited until she ate and her curiosity outweighed her

hunger. "Someone will come soon to see what's happening. Do you want to tell me what you saw in private?"

"Always anxious to keep moving forward," Blu said, chuckling. "I suppose, in this circumstance, I can understand the feeling."

Relaxing, Madeline reached for the caf jug. "Is it something difficult? For me to hear, I mean?" She felt a tremble of fear in her gut. Was something wrong with the babies? She hadn't had time to tell Blu how they had given back her magic, or about the vision of them on her beach. A place that was becoming more than just her centering image.

"Not hard for you to hear, perhaps it is harder for me to say. But I am concerned that the information will mean you are worrying again about who you are able to trust."

A measure of relief replaced the fear. "Blu, why are you hesitating? Are you unsure of what you saw?"

He tucked his hands inside the sleeves of his robe, a familiar action that Madeline knew was a stalling tactic. Blu hadn't decided what he understood about this information. It was unusual that he'd even mentioned it unless he was willing to talk.

"When we were there, on your beach, I saw something about you that concerns me. This is something you would not notice because you cannot see your true self from the outside." Blu paused again and then gave a small nod to himself. "Someone has been using magic to influence your thinking."

Madeline couldn't breathe from panic. If Rekart had placed a spell on her to avoid being recognized as an enemy... She wanted to stand, but her legs were numb. "Who?"

"I do not know," he said.

Angry at yet another barrier, one that she still felt she should have seen, Madeline pushed herself up, and told her legs to stop shaking. "Do you know anything else?"

Blu rose to join her. "It has not been there long, and it is not a strong compulsion. I think it is more of a nudge. It requires a suggestion from outside." He took her arm and followed her lead to the outside. "And it requires that you have a mind to agree with the suggestion."

"I've been pulled between a dozen opinions in the last week," she admitted. "And everyone has been advising me. So, we're back to the problem that I don't know who to trust."

He patted her hand. "You can trust me, and Simon. And it is not necessarily true that this magic is ill intended."

Madeline was doubtful about the last statement. "I can trust Jode," she said. "And Callisra, she might be able to help with her healing magic. Where is she?"

A smile lit Blu's face. "She did not come with us."

Confused, Madeline asked, "Why does that make you happy?"

"She was unable to come because she is with child. The memory of the whole affair of convincing her to stay is what makes me smile."

Madeline felt a surge of happiness with the news. "I'm looking forward to seeing her when this is done."

Blu stopped and turned her to look at him. "I feel some power in what you say. Take that as a good omen. We will overcome this problem, and we will survive for your children to meet hers."

It was a comfort to hear the words. Madeline found herself trying not to question the truth in them. She felt nothing of her magic to indicate that it was true. "Let's join the others. We need to get this over with."

34

*T*he ride to the circle passed in a blur for Madeline, she'd talked to Simon briefly, but mostly she hid in her thoughts. Blu sat beside her on the wagon seat; everyone else rode. The calendar was in the bed of the wagon along with ropes attached to harnesses, and Madeline's throwing knives. The knives were packed into a vest that she could slip on over the harness.

Confusion, hurt, and anger fought for control of her emotions. Confusion over who she could trust and which of the answers they had found was real, resisted her effort to reestablish the calm she'd felt only a short time ago. Hurt that someone she trusted was trying to sway her. And anger that she was so easily fooled.

Blu didn't seem to be worried. Willowvine rode beside them and she was telling the small priest her story. Their discussion was a quiet backdrop to Madeline's turmoil. The child was more chatty with Blu than she'd been with anyone. By the time they arrived at what was now their usual camp, Madeline had forcibly shut down the feelings. They would not help her get the gate sealed, and afterward it would probably not matter.

After they unloaded the wagon, Madeline shrugged into the harness and vest in preparation of placing the calendar in the center of the well. They planned to do that as close to noon as possible to avoid the risk that the being inside would find a way to destroy it. Blu slipped on a second harness and followed Madeline around the circle of stones.

"Rekart is correct that this is a calendar. It is also an altar," he said pointing to the fine channels that ran between the stones now that all they were in the right place. "There must be a need for blood."

Madeline nodded. "Rekart said that there must be a fight. I guess that's where the blood comes from."

Blu took her hand as they stood at the edge of the well. There was no feeling of dread this time. At least, none from the well. Madeline's fear had been building from the time they stepped onto the first stone, and now she was shaking with it.

Quelling the panic, Madeline took a step back. "Let's return to the others. I'll have Springheart and Regis place the calendar." She felt like a coward, but it wasn't going to change her mind.

Blu led her across the stones to the waiting crowd, where Regis and Springheart were already harnessed. They had only brought four harnesses because Madeline didn't want to risk everyone in the ceremony. If she could have found confidence that she didn't need help, Madeline would have happily kept everyone outside the circle where it was safe. Or at least, safer than it was on the stones.

Anticipating the worst, she watched the two men cross the stones and kneel at the edge. From this angle, it looked like they were praying, but she saw the calendar snap into place, the standing poles quivering as it settled. Regis and Springheart stood and took a few steps backward. The plan was to have them witness the shadow falling, and then retrieve the calendar.

As the sun passed the high point, Madeline saw the shadows of the twelve poles appear. The passing of the sun made it seem as though the shadows were performing a stately dance, each moving in an arc until they were all lined up and pointing to one stone. From this distance, it was hard to see how close to the last stone they were, but it was one of the last few.

Springheart moved forward to take the calendar from the well. As his hand reached for the closest pole, he jerked backwards. Regis pulled at him and they retreated, as the calendar burst into green flames. The fire consumed the device too quickly to be explained by the age and dryness of the wood. This was magic.

The being in the well had awakened.

Shaking with fear, Madeline waited until the two men reached safety. "Which stone," she asked. "How long do we have?"

"Two days," Regis answered. "The shadow stopped on the second to last stone."

"The army will arrive on the day before battle," Jode said. His voice carried something Madeline had never heard before. Her calm and brave husband was afraid. "They will fight with no time to recover from travel."

Fear retreating in the face of her growing determination, Madeline said, "No they will arrive after we have sealed the gate. It won't matter if they are tired."

"Then you have decided what to sacrifice?" Amberbirch asked, a sickening eagerness in her voice. "You will seal the gate for eternity?"

"I have not chosen. I am not sure that the choice is completely mine yet," Madeline answered.

Amberbirch's eyes narrowed. "You are The Chosen. Of course, the choice is yours."

Determined that she wouldn't be forced into a decision, Madeline held up her hand. "I need solitude." She was almost embarrassed to use the words. It sounded so pompous. "I just need a few minutes."

Turning to find a quiet place in the copse of trees, Madeline saw Willowvine whispering to Blu. The priest was nodding his head at whatever the girl said. Madeline kept walking, hoping that whatever was agitating Willowvine would wait.

She slipped into the clearing between the trees and lowered herself to the ground. Now that the time had come, she needed to be calm and the only way she knew how to do that was to go to her beach. It took only a few breaths for her to find the warmth of the sun. The sand showed no evidence of the violence from the morning. She asked it to show her the scene again, but nothing happened. Settling for the peace she usually got from the visit, Madeline basked in the warmth and the sound of the waves. In moments, she felt the tightness of her soul release.

She still didn't know what to do, but she now felt like she would know the answer when the time was right. She let the vision go and opened her eyes to see Willowvine sitting across from her.

Holding onto the peace she'd gained, Madeline smiled and asked, "Why are you here?"

"Blu said I should talk to you." Willowvine kept her gaze on Madeline's face. "I saw something. He told me what he found on you. The spell."

Madeline quelled the rising fear. In control of her emotions, she asked, "And you saw something about it?"

"It's Amberbirch. She's the one trying to make you do things."

Surprised that she believed the girl, Madeline realized she had expected it. Since last night, she'd wondered how Amberbirch was able to get her way despite Madeline's objections. It had seemed like caring, like a motherly thing to do. She hadn't questioned it. She struggled to get to her feet. "How do you know?"

Willowvine stood in one smooth motion and held her hand out to assist Madeline. "When you were arguing, I saw her magic. Every time you disagreed with her, you glowed. In my vision sight."

35

*M*adeline marched determinedly to the waiting group, checking her weapons as she approached. Amberbirch was standing at the edge of the stone circle. Something flickered in her eyes as Madeline neared. The woman swallowed and took a step backward, almost stumbling onto the stones.

Out of the corner of her eye, Madeline saw Simon and Jode moving to join her and commanded them to stay back. She didn't need distractions.

"Why did you do it?" Madeline asked. There was no time to soften the words. Amberbirch had betrayed her trust, and Madeline needed to know why. It couldn't get in the way of the ceremony.

"What do you mean?" Amberbirch looked over Madeline's shoulder. "You would believe that girl. You've known her for only hours."

Madeline didn't speak. She kept walking forward.

Amberbirch stepped backward.

Calm, perhaps too calm, Madeline tuned out the conversation

behind her. No one was trying to pull her back, so she kept moving. "Why? Did you think that I wouldn't do this without your influence?"

The change in Amberbirch's expression was rapid. Her gaze hardened, and she stopped backing away. "You still think you can find a way to do this without pain. You have no idea what pain is."

Shocked at the bitterness in the words, Madeline stopped advancing. "You think I don't know what it means to kill?"

Amberbirch spat on the stones. "You have never killed without being forced to. I know your history. You kill by instinct, never by plan."

Madeline pulled her knife from the middle pocket of the vest. This one had a suede wrapped tang that allowed her to use it in a fight as well as throw it. Still holding onto the calm, she showed it to Amberbirch. "You're right. I think I should be reluctant to kill on a plan. I've killed enough people to know that I don't like it. Tell me why."

"My son. You would dishonor him by taking the easy path. He died to defend this land. My only son. One I could never replace." The hatred in her eyes wavered as she spoke.

Madeline's mind filled with the pain Amberbirch felt. She had never thought about the sacrifice in that way. Was Amberbirch right? Neither path was easy, but did she have the right to choose the less hard path? Her thoughts were interrupted by the sound of boots on stone. She felt rather than saw movement as Amberbirch stepped closer, then there was pain.

"You are the sacrifice that will seal the gate," Amberbirch rasped.

Madeline's mind could only register movement. Amberbirch started to pull her toward the center, the harness tightened as someone pulled on the rope. Then she was pushed to the side, stumbling holding her hands out to break her fall.

Jode caught her before she landed. Madeline looked up to see Rekart and Regis restraining Amberbirch.

Jode lifted Madeline and carried her to the camp. "It will be fine," he whispered to her.

She looked at her hand where the pain throbbed. Amberbirch had pulled the knife from Madeline's grip, slicing open her palm. "Where is the knife?" Madeline asked.

"She threw it into the well," Blu answered.

Rekart twisted Amberbirch's arm behind her. "We have started the ceremony."

Madeline's hand was dripping blood, and she couldn't be healed. The only real healer they had was now tied and guarded. Springheart tried, but the wound was stubborn. Weakness robbed her of the ability to think clearly. All she could focus on was the blood that Amberbirch had dropped in the well with the knife. "Rekart, do you know if the blood offered needs to come from the sacrifice?" She winced as Jode packed herbs and then a cloth into the wound to stanch the flow. He bound her hand with another strip of material. The bandage stayed clean, so she hoped that the flow was stemmed.

Rekart knelt before her. "No, it does not determine the sacrifice. You still have time to conduct either ceremony. You must do this now. I do not think your blood will satisfy the being for long."

Startled by the information, Madeline looked up, the pain in her hand fading into the background of her consciousness. "I thought you had never heard of the being."

He seemed to search for words to answer. Madeline saw the frustration on his face increase the look of age. She was surprised that there was no feeling of distrust in her mind. "I have not, but now that I know about it, I have been thinking of the relationship between the being and the ceremony. I believe we are attempting to lull the being with the blood. While it is focused on that, we have time to seal the gate. The gate is like a door, the creature its guardian."

Feeling the sense in his words, Madeline stood, keeping her damaged hand tucked tight to her waist. "Then we need to go to the well. We need to complete the ceremony."

Jode held her shoulders as he looked into her eyes. "Madeline, have you decided what to do? If you need a life, you can have mine."

She wished that she could say yes, that she'd found a way to seal the gate. But there was no clear answer. There was no path she could see, but she had to approach the well. It was calling her, as though ready for the battle, eager even. Rekart may have been right about the blood. She'd felt the world shift slightly as the words were said. She also knew that blood wasn't enough, yet. "Let's just go to the center," she said. "Someone needs to watch Amberbirch, but I don't want to do this alone. I need help. I need my friends."

Blu slipped out of the harness and pulled his robes around his small frame. "I think I will only be in the way if it comes to a battle. I will watch the woman."

Relieved, Madeline said, "Willowvine can stay back too."

The girl was slipping into a harness. "I have to come. You will need me to know the truth."

Madeline shook her head, fear cooling her from the inside out. "No, we only have four harnesses. You stay here."

Willowvine's face burned with purpose. "No, this must be you and me. Rekart and Jode will come. The others can stay and guard her. Can't you hear that voice?"

Madeline could hear it louder now. She couldn't make out words, but there were screams, and something under that noise. Someone was chanting... no singing. It was a sound of joy. "Can anyone else hear it?"

No one admitted to hearing the sound. Madeline didn't believe that they could lie about it. Now that she'd acknowledge the sound, it was growing. The singing was drawing her from this side, and doing something horrific to whoever was on the other side. "Jode, you and Rekart get into the harnesses. Everyone else stays here."

She walked over to where Amberbirch was struggling against the ropes that bound her. Pity warred with anger as Madeline crouched to talk to her. "You may have taken my choice away, but I swear that I will seal that gate. When we are done, you and I will have a long talk about your methods."

"I will have no life when you are done," she snarled. "My life began to die with my son. Now my daughter is dead, and I have no one. Like that girl and Springheart, I will be thrown to the winds. If I have made you seal it forever, then I will gladly give up my life."

Pity won the battle. "I am sorry to hear about your daughter. But surely you will not be cast out."

"I have no family." The words came on a sob that broke Madeline's heart.

"I cannot forgive you for what you've done, but I am sorry," she said. Not waiting for a reply, she turned to see the others were ready. The thought brought bitter humor to her. How could anyone be ready for this?

Looking around her, she noticed that they were no longer alone. Men lined the hills around the bowl of the well. The army had arrived early. "Jode, how will they know to stay way until..." She couldn't express the fears that flooded her.

Springheart answered. "They aren't waiting for you. They are waiting for the signs that the gate is opening. If we succeed, we may have to inform them that they are not needed."

Madeline turned to look toward the well. "When we succeed, not if. We need to go. Tie the ends of the ropes to the wagon. Make sure that Amberbirch is kept away from us."

She started walking to the well, taking the circular approach. She wasn't sure why, but it felt like part of the ceremony, as if there were no other reason for the makers to have arranged them in that order. After a few steps, the others caught up and kept her pace. Before, this path seemed so clear, a message, a place to find an answer; now, it was a path to death. As much as she wanted to find another answer, Madeline knew in her bones that someone would die before they were finished. And by choosing her companions, she'd picked a sacrifice.

36

Springheart watched as four people he considered friends walked away into danger without him. It pained him because he had never stood by before when someone walked into a fight. And more, it was the first time he had friends. As an elf, he frightened people. The reputation of his race for berserker fighting was deserved, but it got between individual elves and other people. He'd come to terms with that in the years he'd been out in the world. Now these people, even the Scree, were his friends. It was difficult sometimes to know how to act with them, but it was worth the effort.

Hearing a noise behind him, Springheart turned to see Amberbirch still struggling against the ropes that bound her. Regis was sitting on the wagon seat, turned so that he could observe the woman struggle and talk to Simon at the same time. Blu was meditating, holding ribbons in his hands as he muttered something that Springheart could only hope were spells to ensure their success.

Ignoring the soldiers arranged around them, like another circle of the passage to the gate, he sat across from the elven woman who been leading them through the discovery of clues.

"Do you want some water?" he asked, unwilling to start talking about what he really wanted to know.

She looked at him without the usual sneer. No one else had noticed that, the way she'd always looked at him, as though he was lower than dirt. Willowvine hadn't seemed to notice, but then he had played the same game of denial, so it was unlikely that the girl was oblivious. Self-preservation wasn't just about physical safety.

"No, it will not be long now," she said, licking her lips. "If that woman is successful, then we will live. If not, then we will all die." Her struggles became smaller. Springheart hoped that meant she had given up trying to escape.

They were speaking quietly, but Springheart did not want to be overheard. He glanced around and was relieved to see no one paying attention. Regis had turned away to watch the activity in the circle. He was still talking to Simon, it sounded as though he was explaining the purpose of the stones.

"Why did you take that risk?"

Amberbirch stopped struggling and gave Springheart an appraising look. "I had no reason to trust that woman. She was not willing to do the hard thing. She would have simply postponed the inevitable."

He didn't want to argue, but he did want to understand Amberbirch's motives. "Madeline will do what is needed. A thousand years is a long time to find another answer."

She laughed and started to struggle again. "Do you think that there have been no other attempts?"

Surprised, he asked her to explain.

"I kept some knowledge to myself. Some of it was useless, it was nothing that would help. Other information… well perhaps I should not have kept that from her."

Springheart felt anger burn. He slammed his fist into the ground to stop him from slamming it into her face. "You put us all at risk. The information you held back could have helped make this, if not easier, faster. We could have been done by now. The army would not have been mobilized."

She stopped moving. "No, it couldn't. We needed the enemy and the child. Until those two arrived the ceremony could not be conducted."

He leaned in to make sure no one heard. It would only confuse things for Regis, or Blu, to know that Amberbirch had such detailed information. He hated what she had done, but she was an elf, and one without family. That made her the same as him and Willowvine. "What else do you know?"

She leaned toward him. "The ceremony is not totally in the hands of The Chosen. Her role was to uncover the answers. The Chosen has three companions. The missing one is the crone. One of those will start the ceremony, one of them will end it."

"You are the crone? You weren't trying to kill Madeline?" Shock froze him. "You wanted her blood to start the ceremony. Do you think that means she is the sacrifice?"

Amberbirch looked over his shoulder. He knew that she could see the four people who must be approaching the center of the circle by now. "I am not certain," she said. "That was not clear in any of the books I found. But blood was needed to start the ceremony, and blood will be needed to complete it. I do not care whose blood. She does."

He leaned closer. "She will not fail us. I have seen her be merciful. It was not at the expense of what was needed."

She leaned closer to him and he moved in to hear what she was going add.

Amberbirch opened her mouth to speak, and then reached out and wrapped her hands around his throat. She'd stopped moving because she'd broken free.

Calmly he reached to pull her hands away. She was an old woman and he was in his prime, there was no way she could hurt him. But her grip was stronger than he expected, strong enough to keep him from crying out.

Weakness robbed him of the ability to pull her hands away, or to get Regis' attention. Her grip strengthened and his eyes start to bulge. His face felt swollen. His lungs burned for air and the world started to fade at the edges.

The last thing he heard as the world disappeared was Amber-birch's voice, "I will not let her be weak. The gate will be closed permanently."

The last thing he felt was her hands leaving his throat.

37

At the center of the circle, Madeline stood waiting. She felt empty of all emotions since Amberbirch revealed herself. There was no doubt any more, she trusted the three people with her, and the three behind. She couldn't feel any fear either. There was only the well, and the question of what she would sacrifice.

"Is there still a chance to avoid a death?" she asked Rekart.

"You have already given it blood and the battle. There is only the sacrifice. If you want to change the events, I cannot predict what will happen."

Unsurprised, she turned to Willowvine. "Now that you are here, do you know why?"

The girl was dangerously close the edge of the well; she was hanging from the stretched rope of her harness. Madeline feared that the knots would loosen from the end at the wagon. Willowvine turned to look at Madeline, eyes shining. "The truth is in the song. Can you hear it?"

Madeline stepped beside Willowvine, uneasy at the closeness of the abyss. The screams still created a backdrop, but the song was stronger. Joy filled the words. It was the being who had threatened them.

"Yes, but I can't understand the words." The sounds raised the tiny hairs all over her body. She looked at Rekart and Jode. The Scree was looking into the well, but Madeline could tell from his calm that he couldn't hear the voice. Jode was standing guard as he always did. His sword was in his hand, he was staring at her, and she could feel his love holding her strong.

Willowvine stepped back from the edge, her face still lit with some emotion that Madeline couldn't understand. "He is singing a song of the gate. The story of the gate. It is the truth of the event."

Truth. Madeline had never thought of it as an emotion, but that was what shone from Willowvine's eyes. "What does it say?"

"That the gate was created by the gods," she said. "That a god lives in the center of the gate. That only a sacrifice from this world can seal the gate and kill the god." Willowvine frowned, the glow of truth fading. "Can a god be killed?"

"Do you hear it as true?" Madeline hoped that the answer would be no. That the creature was not a god. If it was, there would be worshipers; there would be repercussions.

Willowvine looked at the well. "I do not know about the god part, but when we seal the gate, that being will die. That voice will be stilled."

Madeline couldn't find it within her to feel the loss that Willowvine was clearly experiencing at the thought of killing the creature in the well. They were only one act from sealing the gate. The sacrifice. As much as she wanted to avoid it, there would be two deaths, just like the vision in the sand. One of her friends and the beast. Looking at Willowvine, fear chilled Madeline from the heart out. She'd seen that look before. On fanatics. "It has to be an unwilling sacrifice."

Willowvine shook her head and laughed. "I am not going to jump into the well. I have many more things to do with my life."

Relieved, Madeline turned to listen again. Jode rushed toward her. She had time to notice his harness was no longer tied to the wagon. Then he raised his sword and sliced her rope free. She staggered back as he ran past to release the others. "What..."

He returned to stand beside her, facing the edge of the circle. "You will need to be mobile more than you need to be safe." He pointed, and Madeline saw Amberbirch was running toward them, a blade in her hands. Madeline pulled her own knives from the vest and yelled at Rekart and Willowvine to return to the wagon. Neither obeyed. Rekart stood with Jode. Willowvine was a blur of movement as she ran to intercept Amberbirch. They clashed, but the older woman was the stronger and she pushed Willowvine to the ground as she ran toward Madeline.

Unwieldy because of the babies, Madeline moved away from the well. While she still had time, she was determined not to fall in because she fought too close to the edge. She could see Regis and Simon running to join the fight. Springheart trailing behind, hurt.

Amberbirch was screaming as she ran. Tossing a small bag toward Madeline, she raised her sword to attack. Jode stepped between the two women. The small bag hit him in the chest and he collapsed.

Madeline's heart froze. She threw her knife at Amberbirch as she yelled to Simon to go to Jode.

Her heartbeat sounded too slow to be real. Between beats, Amberbirch crossed half the distance between them as the knife flew toward her. "Regis, protect Rekart," she ordered. The knife flew wide and Madeline's heart beat again. Now there was only Amberbirch to deal with. Springheart was gaining speed, but he was definitely injured. Madeline knew that she would have to fight the elven woman, this time she could show no mercy. Madness had taken Amberbirch's reason, and elves fought to the end. That's what she had been told more than once.

Knowing it would not cut through the insanity, Madeline still found herself compelled to speak, "What have you done? Do want to stop us from sealing the gate?" Her words came out in a scream of rage. Amberbirch was not the only one who would fight to the death.

The woman kept coming without answering. The words spewing from Amberbirch's mouth were rhythmic, incoherent, and powerful. Madeline could feel the magic building. She moved away from where the others stood.

Changing direction, Amberbirch stumbled, the words didn't stop as she forced herself up from the stones, leaving a smear of blood where her skin had been rubbed away from the force of her movement.

The stumble allowed Springheart to come closer.

Madeline's heart beat again.

Across from her, she saw a flash of Blu's robes. He was running to the line of soldiers.

As Madeline's heart beat again, Amberbirch reached her. The words stopped, and the world went silent. Whatever the spell was supposed to do, it had no effect on Madeline's ability to fight. She slashed at Amberbirch as soon as the woman was within reach.

Amberbirch lunged, but she had no skill with a blade. The movement unbalanced her. Madeline stepped aside and regretted the shortness of her own blade as she had to let Amberbirch pass. Going too close would give the woman a chance to stab at the babies.

Recovering much faster than Madeline expected, Amberbirch turned to engage again. Madeline could see that the weapon was already taking its toll on her. The weight of the sword was straining her wrist, it wouldn't be long before the blade would be touching the ground.

Madeline sidestepped and let Amberbirch pass again without attack.

The silence was unnerving. Madeline couldn't keep track of where everyone was. She couldn't take time to scan the area long enough to locate her friends. She had to keep her focus on Amberbirch. The only reason to look away was to make sure she wasn't about to step over the edge of the well. Despite conscious effort, the slight concavity to the stone circle kept pushing her to the center.

Amberbirch was panting now. The rage in her eyes still blazed, but her body didn't have the stamina to fight much longer. Madeline turned sideways to avoid another clumsy attack.

Now she was facing the well, and feeling much more sure that she could out-wait Amberbirch's energy. She fought the temptation to look around her. Inattention could change the outcome of the most uneven fight.

Her opponent stopped moving and stood gasping, drenched in sweat, body exhausted. Madeline started to tell her to drop her sword and stop, when the exhaustion in Amberbirch's eyes was replaced by something that wasn't tired, that wasn't befuddled with rage, that wasn't Amberbirch.

Madeline tried to back up farther, needing distance to feel safe, but after a few steps she felt a barrier push back. The spell Amberbirch had been casting had been an enclosure. As Madeline watched, her opponent moved toward her. The first steps were jerky, but whatever controlled Amberbirch's body mastered it rapidly.

Breathing out the fear that seemed to flood her mind, Madeline threw the first of her remaining knives. One lodged itself in Amberbirch's side. It didn't stop her progress. Blood soaked her robe, but she just kept moving.

Madeline aimed her next knife at the sword arm, hoping to create enough damage that the creature couldn't use the weapon. It missed.

She had three knives left. Throwing the next two, Madeline made contact with both, one stuck in the shoulder and the other in the belly. The creature stumbled from the force of the contact, but recovered and continued advancing.

One knife left, and it was too short to use effectively against the sword. Madeline couldn't rely on lack of skill. Whatever Amberbirch had let into her spirit, would just keep coming. It would keep moving her toward the well, it would pull her in by sheer force if she couldn't think of how to attack.

She took a step backward for every forward step. A bizarre waltz that only bought her a little time. She had no illusion that the creature would tire. The only plan she could think of was to use the well as her weapon. If she could trick it, and avoid being pulled in, Madeline could drop the creature in the well, find a way to collapse the enclosure spell, and get back to sealing the gate. The only way she could imagine that the plan would work was to damage Amberbirch's body in a way that it couldn't move, then tip it in the well.

Madeline started to move faster, not quite a run, but enough to get the creature moving. She edged closer to the well until they were standing on the last ring of stones. The creature was pushing Amberbirch's body past its abilities. The sword arm was shaking with the effort of holding it up, but the sword still pointed at Madeline. As it moved, Madeline saw how the feet dragged.

Shaking with exhaustion herself, Madeline could imagine the toll that was being taken on Amberbirch's older body. She shifted her weight forward, bouncing on the balls of her feet. Leaning to her right, Madeline watched the creature move to intercept. As soon as it seemed committed, Madeline shifted left, away from the well.

Amberbirch followed her, body twisting to match the move, feet dragging. As her body finished the turn, Amberbirch collapsed on the stone, the sword clattered out of reach. The creature kept trying to crawl toward Madeline, but her plan had worked. A torn hamstring had the same effect as cutting the strings on a puppet.

Madeline walked toward the body, avoiding the grasping hands. It wasn't Amberbirch any longer. She had to drag it to the well. To hope this was sacrifice enough. One push and the body rolled over the edge.

Madeline backed away from the well, waiting for the feeling of the barrier, but it didn't come, instead, voices cut the silence, hands caught her as she collapsed.

38

"*M*adeline."

She heard Jode's voice calling. She wanted to wake up, but she was too deep in the tunnel. How did she get here? Madeline reached to her side trying to feel the walls, but no matter how much she stretched, she couldn't touch them.

Was she falling?

There was no sensation of falling.

There was no sensation at all.

"Madeline."

This time the voice was different. There was an echo. Jode's voice was frightened, she'd never heard that before. The echo was inviting, it was familiar. Madeline tried to change position. It had sounded like Jode's voice came from above, the other from below. As if wishing made it possible, she felt herself standing on something she couldn't see.

"Madeline."

This time Jode's voice was the echo. He was a long way off. The other voice was in front of her. She recognized it and wished to be back with Jode. This time wishing didn't make it so. The creature in the center of the well stood in front of her. She was absolutely sure of it, even though there was nothing to see.

"Madeline," Jode's voice was almost inaudible now.

The creature kept talking, its voice a seductive whisper, "Welcome to my world. Is it not beautiful?"

Visions of rolling hills covered in wildflowers appeared. A flurry of birds broke from the branches of a huge tree.

Afraid that acknowledging his presence would make it real, or keep her here, Madeline said nothing. She tried to go to her beach. If she could take her spirit there, then maybe she could return to her body. She couldn't raise any sensations. This place held no physical properties for her to use.

"Thank you for that first taste, but it was not sufficient to the ceremony." It waited, but Madeline kept her vow. The last call from Jode still echoing in her heart. When it became obvious that she wasn't going to speak, the voice chuckled. "Did you like the way I concealed the answers? How I stole the information from the students as they were taught the ceremony? I have a little power in that world. Of course, I could not stop The Chosen from finding the answers, learning what to throw into the well with me. I almost did, though. One more day."

The urge to answer was almost overwhelming. Madeline pressed her lips together to stop the words escaping. Why was this creature not distracted with the sacrifice? Why was it so strong still?

"The first sacrifice has closed the gate, and I have you here, so you cannot complete the final step and seal it. I will open the gate again."

Hope started to drive the fear. The creature was gloating. She needed to find a way to get back to Jode. There was a way to stop him, and she would find it, but not here. There was nothing she could do here.

"I save lives," the voice said. "I don't send these people here to die."

Madeline chose to believe Rekart's version of the story. In the silences, she could hear Jode's voice calling, the pain tearing at her.

"The gate is not locked," the creature said. "I will open it soon and then… you will die knowing you failed."

Madeline stopped listening to the voice. She strained for Jode's call. She answered, him with her own thought. "Jode."

His voice became stronger. She answered again. "Jode, don't let me go."

Her name came through stronger, the creature's voice fading.

She opened her eyes.

The sun was warm. Jode's arms cradled her and she was safe.

Relieved that her plan had worked, Madeline kissed Jode and wiped tears from his cheeks before getting to her feet. "We need to do more. Another sacrifice."

"Please come away from the edge, my love," Jode said.

She allowed him to draw her a few steps away from the well, but stood her ground when he tried to take her farther.

"I have to finish this," she said. "There is something that we need to throw in the well."

Regis stepped up. "I will gladly give something. Perhaps my magic?"

Springheart offered his life, but Madeline said it was a thing not a person. When Rekart started to offer his magical powders, Madeline called for silence.

Trying to think through the selfless offers was impossible. There were too many people there. "I need to do this alone. All of you go back to the wagon. No, even better, go join the army on the hill."

Willowvine took her arm. "Madeline, you cannot do this alone. I know that is the truth."

Frustrated, Madeline placed her hands on her belly, feeling the movement of the babies. "Willowvine, can you tell who needs to be here? I can't believe that all of us are needed."

P. A. WILSON

The girl looked at each of the people standing with them. As she made her assessment, Madeline fussed with the harness. Her knife vest was empty. and the harness was no longer attached to the wagon so she wasn't taking a risk by removing them. Her certainty wavered as she watched Jode start to protest. But he didn't speak, so she opted for more freedom of movement.

"This requires three people," Willowvine announced. "Spring-heart, me, and you."

Anguished that she had no way of verifying the statement, Madeline allowed herself a small satisfaction that the crowd of people would be thinned. Jode would be safe, and Simon. The two people she cared the most about. "Then everyone else needs to go," she said, running to give Jode a final kiss. "I'll be success-ful. I swear we will see these children grow to adulthood." She remembered her vision on the journey to rescue Lee. "They will be beautiful, and red haired, and full of mischief."

Jode kissed the mound of her belly. "Do not die, or I will be very angry."

She laughed, although she felt no joy. "Go and take care of the others. And make sure that the army doesn't interrupt us."

He kissed her again and handed her his sword. "Just in case," he said before gathering everyone and leading them away.

Madeline turned to the two people waiting for her to tell them the plan. The plan that didn't exist. "Let's have a look in the well. I get the feeling the answer is there." She looked at Willowvine. "Can you see the truth in something I say, even if I don't know if I am right?"

Willowvine frowned. "Sometimes, with some people. Say two things that I do not know. One of them must be a lie."

Madeline thought hard for both the lie and the truth. She was desperate to know if her guess was real. If she told a truth and her guess, and Willowvine couldn't read her, then she would not know if the guess was a truth. "I have flown within a machine from one country to another. I have traveled under the sea in a machine." Both of those should sound fantastic enough to be lies.

Willowvine laughed. "You must tell me about this flying machine. You have not been inside a machine that travels under water."

Relief flooded Madeline so quickly it left her lightheaded. "It worked. I am sure we do not have to give anyone's life to the well, one death was sufficient."

Willowvine confirmed Madeline's guess, "It is true, but I think it is not the complete truth."

39

"Madeline," the creature called again.

Madeline stood motionless, waiting to learn if her spirit was to leave her. When she realized that it was not going to happen, she stepped cautiously to the edge of the well. Turning to Springheart and Willowvine, she asked, "Do you hear it?"

They nodded and sat together on the edge. "Join us, so that you are less likely to fall in," Springheart said.

Madeline sat, her legs dangling over the edge.

"Madeline, are you listening?" The seductive tone was back in the voice.

Now that she was safely in the physical world, Madeline was sure she could answer. "What do you want?"

A chuckle echoed from the well. "It is good to hear your voice, Chosen One."

Madeline hated that expression. Too many bad movies in her past had used it. "Aren't you too busy trying to open the gate for a chat?"

There was a pause. Madeline pictured a shadow crouched over a trapdoor, struggling to pull it open.

"The first sacrifice was strong. Even with my influence draining her power, the elven woman is able to hold the gate. That will not be true once the passage starts."

Madeline pulled herself back from the edge and stood, tugging at Springheart and Willowvine. Panic edged her voice as she said, "It's getting closer." Her body started to shake. "It's just trying to delay. It was supposed to be distracted by the sacrifice."

Springheart took her hands. "That may be true," he said quietly. "But you must keep speaking until we hear what it needs. You must ask questions that Willowvine can assess. We can still seal the gate and hope that the creature will die."

Willowvine drew away a little. "Madeline is right, the gate will open soon, and that creature is just stalling."

Taking control of her fear, Madeline approached the well again. "It seems to me that the answer is simple. The ceremony doesn't need another sacrifice, at least not something physical."

"Do not try to trick me, Chosen One." Fury boiled above the surface of the well, like the heat shimmer on a road.

Madeline knew that she'd come close to the answer. "It has to be something intangible." She kept her eyes on Willowvine; the girl was nodding. "Something that I value."

"Do you think I will tell you how to bring about my death?" The voice was definitely closer now. "You may be The Chosen, but you are not intelligent. Those children you bear are better dead in the coming battle than they are being raised by you."

Madeline laughed at the feeble attempt to anger her. "Well, children are resilient." As the words left her mouth, she realized that the entity was trying to distract her again. Something was happening and she was missing it. Determined not to allow it to win, she started scanning the area. There was nothing in the hills around, nothing behind her. When she turned back to the well, she saw it. The shimmer she'd seen earlier had thickened. As she watched, it formed tendrils.

"Are you trying to join us?" she asked as casually as she could manage. While she waited for the response, she pointed it out to the other two and motioned them to move away.

"I do not come into your world," the voice whispered.

Madeline looked at Willowvine for confirmation. The girl nodded, and then a look of shock crossed her face as she moved toward the well.

Springheart grabbed her and pulled. He slowed her progress, but she still inched toward the well. Madeline could see a tendril of the shimmer wrapped around Willowvine's ankle. Another was reaching for Springheart. As she lifted Jode's sword from the pavement and raised it to slice at the tendril, Madeline side-stepped another that was slithering across the stones in her direction.

The sword had no effect on the shimmer, it simple passed through to bounce off the stones. She tossed it to the side and joined Springheart in his efforts to pull the girl away.

It didn't help. Madeline was losing the battle to save her friends, a battle she hadn't noticed until it was too late.

It was her fault. She didn't know what to do to close the gate. She didn't know how to save these two innocent people. The creature was winning.

Willowvine's feet dangled over the edge of the well. The only thing stopping her from dropping to her death was the grip Madeline and Springheart had on her arms.

"Let me go," Willowvine said, as she tried to wiggle out of their grasp. "I'm not worth it. Let it have me."

"No," Madeline screamed the word. Her vision grayed and she felt reason slipping away. She only had her magic to rely on. She closed her eyes and slipped onto her beach. She wasn't alone. The twins were there. Rage at the loss of their future; fury at all the losses she'd faced since coming to Cartref tore at her. The children giggled, but this time it just fueled her anger. She held her hands out in front of her. She focused her rage into a ball of light. It spun in her hands and started spitting sparks. She could feel her feet slipping in the real world. Willowvine would be inside the well now.

Madeline looked at the children. They were fading. Terror that she was losing them, snapped her back into the world. Willowvine was only visible because her hand was in Springheart's grasp. He was lying on the ground struggling to stop her falling.

Madeline heard laughter coming from inside the well. Her world went dark. She screamed all of the loss she'd felt, all of her anger, all of her despair, and hurled the ball of light into the well.

Thunder shook the world.

Madeline staggered as she bent to grasp Springheart to stop him from falling into the well. He still held Willowvine.

Her ears rang from the thunder, but her throat was burning with the scream she couldn't stop. She strained to pull him away. Eyes on the well, she saw Willowvine reaching for the edge of it. She fell back as the tension of holding the girl released before she could adjust.

Everyone safe.

Madeline crawled to the edge of the well. Trying to send her magic in to see if they were successful. She felt nothing. She had no magic.

Sounds were coming back to her and she realized that Willowvine was talking. Madeline focused on her words.

"You did it. The well is sealed."

Madeline's world went black.

40

*W*hen she woke, Madeline was in the back of the wagon, lying on a pile of cloaks. Jode was sitting beside her, looking down at her. When he saw her eyes open, his face lit up. "Welcome back, Chosen One."

She struggled to sit. "Never call me that again."

He laughed and called out to the others that she was awake. "You sealed the gate. You saved Willowvine and Springheart. Now I am taking you home and never letting you leave the house."

She couldn't argue with him. Madeline was willing to give up adventures for the safety of her house. "Do we have to stop at the library?" she asked. Knowing that they couldn't leave for home tonight, but not wanting the memories of Amberbirch to haunt her.

"Only overnight. The commanders of the armies will want to meet with you and hear the story. There will be scribes to record the momentous events. I am sorry, but I believe we will get little sleep tonight." He sounded more proud of her than regretful.

She moved to sit in his lap and snuggle. "As long as we can head for home tomorrow, I'll stay up and celebrate all night."

By the time they reached the library, the building was bustling with people preparing for their guests. Tents for the leaders were arranged in the clearing. The main body of the army was already on its way back to wherever it came from. Madeline bathed and changed into her only clean dress. A servant promised to have all of her clothes cleaned and packed for the morning. As she descended the stairs, Madeline heard the sound of many voices where there were usually only a few. It made the building seem alive. Peace and contentment filled her, replacing the tension and fear of the last few months.

She grabbed a bun and cheese from the kitchen and walked toward the voices. There were strangers gathered in the research room. Jode stood to the side, Springheart and Willowvine stood together in front of four elven men. No one stopped her from entering, so she slipped in to join Jode. He wrapped an arm around her and held a finger to his lips.

Madeline paid attention to the man standing at the window. Shocked, she realized they were laying a judgment on the two elves.

"You acquitted yourselves honorably. If you had families, they would be proud, but you do not," he said, voice stern and in conflict with the words. "We have heard your record of the events. We have considered our choices. Springheart, you may continue to act as a liaison between the elves and the world." He waited for Springheart to thank them for their wisdom and step away to join Madeline and Jode.

The man turned to Willowvine. "Child, we will give you one more opportunity."

Madeline's magic was gone but she only needed her instinct to know this wasn't going to be pleasant.

Willowvine stood straight, defiance drawing her tall. "I will not tell you where my friends live."

"Then we must exile you," the man said. "Because of your part in sealing the gate, we will allow you time to leave the elven lands. Please do not take more than a week."

Furious at the betrayal, Madeline stepped forward. "No, you should be grateful. Willowvine saved lives, she..." Madeline trailed off. The man was staring at her as if she were an errant child.

Willowvine took Madeline's arm and drew her back. "It's our way, Madeline. It is going to be fine. This was mercy."

The men picked up their cloaks and left the room, each thanking Madeline for her heroic work.

"You can come and live with us," Madeline said to Willowvine.

Springheart offered Madeline a chair. "I think it will be better if she stays with me. I will not accept their offer. You are right, they should have been grateful."

Willowvine looked surprised. "No, we will visit with Madeline. I wish to see these children who are so eager to make us know them."

"You are welcome to stay as long as you like," Jode said before Madeline could voice the same invitation.

Willowvine had tears in her eyes when she thanked them. "And what will we do when we leave?" she added.

Springheart grinned. "We will find our fortunes in the world. You will be amazed at the things you will see."

Madeline left them to talk about their plans and walked with Jode to the kitchen. The warmth and activity soothed her. Blu was sitting with Simon, drinking wine, and talking.

She asked after Callisra as she sat.

"Morning sickness," Simon said. "I almost didn't come, but she ordered me to leave. Fingers crossed she'll be past it by the time we get home. How are the babies?"

She rubbed the mound of her belly. "Quiet now, but I wish I knew why they were so... I don't know... active before."

Blu asked permission to touch her, and Madeline moved her hands away. As the priest made contact, warmth flowed through her. Blu was giving her some of his energy. She would have told him to stop, but she was grateful for his generosity.

"There is nothing special about them now," Blu said. "Well, nothing other than the fact that they are your children. I think they were an agent of the prophecy. But they are healthy and will be wonderful children."

Happy with the news, Madeline put her cup on the table. "I know we have to stay for the feast, but can we leave right after? I don't want to spend another minute in the presence of the kind of people who would exile a child for being an orphan. Even if we only travel for a few hours."

Jode drew her into his embrace. "Yes, we will leave as soon as we can pack the wagons. And as soon as we can do so without giving insult. I would not stoop to their level."

Wrapped in his arms, Madeline felt the world shift. She lost the feeling of urgency that had clung to her since she'd stepped through the tree. Suddenly she felt like she was just a person, and not someone responsible for the wellbeing of the whole world.

WANT MORE?

Willowvine and Springheart receive a mysterious contract to locate a vital artifact. Use the QR code to grab your copy of The Eleven Stones: Family and save the elves.

Sneak peek next.

* * *

If you enjoyed reading End of the Tunnel, please consider helping other readers to find the story by leaving a review.

CHAPTER 1

*W*illowvine stuffed her black scarf into her backpack. This job wasn't likely to go wrong, but she didn't want to be recognized, and the scarf would cover everything that revealed she was an elf. The guild defined legal a little differently from the way the law did. Even so, if she got caught it wouldn't be sure that she'd walk free.

"Why does the guild always send us on these kinds of jobs?" she asked Springheart.

Looking over, she saw him chuckling as he prepared his own pack. In the five years they'd been working as a team for the courier's guild, they'd retrieved a lot of stolen items. The guild was always clear that the items had already been stolen, so taking them back wasn't a crime. Willowvine figured if they were such a special team, maybe they should get more of a fee. When they had more savings, she'd be able to convince Springheart to start their own guild, one that was actually friendly to elves rather than indifferent at best.

Springheart picked up his cloak before he answered. He gave her that look. The one that said she should know the answer, but when she didn't speak, he shrugged and said, "Because we are the best at it. We get in and out fast and quiet. It helps to have your ability to know if anyone is lurking."

Willowvine smiled and shrugged the pack on. "Like we did at the gate between worlds? Saving all of Cartref and then being exiled without so much as a thank you."

"I don't know why you expected any different." Springheart didn't meet her eyes. He paid attention to getting his cloak folded just right. Willowvine knew he was hiding his own disappointment. Just because he didn't talk about it didn't mean he agreed with the way the elves treated orphans.

She knew that people didn't lose their prejudices easily. "I guess it's not that much different from how they treated the scree who helped us. He was different too. Although, I guess, it's been a while since any scree acted on a blood feud, maybe they are losing their warrior culture."

A lot of the beings had changed in the last five years. It was like everyone sensed that the only danger of war was from internal pressure. Without the threat of an invasion, it was possible to live peacefully.

It was time to go and she didn't want to be overheard talking about her plans in the street. There would be people around, there always were, and she didn't want to start an argument if Springheart didn't agree. She took one last look. Their room was tidy. The two beds always made because Springheart believed that keeping their home neat would keep their minds clear. She didn't care. The room was small enough that it didn't take much to deal with. And it meant the landlady stayed out of their business.

They walked to the job side by side. Willowvine waited for a good time to broach the subject of her plans. It was harder than she thought. Maybe she should just tell him despite being in a public place. "I've been thinking." Then she stalled. Springheart didn't really like change, and this was a big one. He glanced over at her, but didn't say anything.

"About our next jobs." She hoped that he would ask. It was too hard to just speak, and she couldn't just blurt it out. They arrived at the job before she could think of a way to say what she needed to say.

The house was dark as promised. Their job was to retrieve a ledger that the tenant had stolen from a rival. Willowvine closed her eyes while Springheart pulled out the ropes they'd use to scale the walls. Her magic wasn't warning her that anyone was thinking about any danger, or that anyone was particularly alert, so it was probably safe. She knew Springheart would want it that way. He liked safe jobs. She preferred a little risk to make things fun.

"It's clear," she whispered. "After, I don't want to just go back to our room." She thought maybe a mug of beer would help her bring the subject up again.

"You want to talk about our next jobs," Springheart said. "Sure, we can talk about anything when this one is done."

She nodded and took the rope he'd coiled to loop over her shoulder. There was a wall to climb and a yard to cross. And then a house wall to climb before she reached the window. For the first time, she was going on her own. It would be her going to the room where the ledger was hidden according to a servant they'd bribed. This was the part that always made her tense, the time when everything could go wrong. The point where they didn't know if the information was good, or if someone was betraying them.

Knowing that Springheart wouldn't be there to cover her back made it worse. Her sense for peril had never let them down before. She was just waiting for the day when it did. She knew that if they moved fast, they would be fine, but Springheart was always worried about being safe. This time he wouldn't be there to do that.

Springheart looked up at the wall and nodded. She took a few steps back and ran toward the wall to gain enough momentum to leap to the top. This was what he'd meant when he'd said they were the best at it. Elves were able to get into places that other species found impossible.

They went over the wall together and landed silently on the grass that surrounded the house. There was no other security, but there was still a possibility of someone seeing them. Springheart tapped her shoulder and they ran to the house, coming to a stop in the shadows of the overhang. Looking up, she saw that the house was going to be a lot easier than the wall. There were trellises and ledges within easy reach.

Willowvine knew that Springheart kept watch for her as she scaled to the third-floor window. It wasn't the same as him being there beside her, but it was a comfort.

Perching on the ledge, she looked into the room. The curtains were open. So far, their source was coming through. Peeking inside, she saw a desk, a set of straight-backed chairs, and a bookshelf. The only light was what filtered in through the window, more than sufficient for elven eyes.

A quick glance at Springheart before she started to open the window showed him scanning the yard, trusting that she would do her job. Sliding a metal tool from inside her jacket, Willowvine placed it between the window and the frame. A jiggle of the bar shifted the window and gave her hope that it would slide up without noise. She prised the window up slowly, using the tool to prop it open as soon as there was enough room for her to slip inside.

The ledger was supposed to be inside a desk drawer. If she could get the drawer open, then she'd take the ledger and join Springheart. If she couldn't, or anything went wrong, she'd drop something to get his attention and he'd climb up and help. She hated thinking through these details, but if she were successful, it would help boost her argument when she talked to him later about their future. A future where elven orphans were respected not ignored.

Willowvine moved to the desk. There were ten drawers. She ignored the center drawer; it was too shallow to hold the target. A tug at the others revealed that they were all locked. As much as she wanted this over with, Willowvine knew that she had to go slowly and leave no trace. Pulling picks out of her pocket, she started with the bottom drawers. They opened easily, but didn't contain the ledger. She kept picking locks until she found what she needed in the top right-hand drawer. As she pulled the ledger out a noise came from outside the room.

SPRINGHEART KEPT his focus on the surrounding yard. If anyone decided to take a late-night stroll on the grounds, they might get trapped. The best way to get this kind of job done was fast. The conditions were perfect. It was calm tonight. Their inside man had assured the guild that the owners would be away. The servants were in the house, but they wouldn't move from their common room.

Assurances were fine, but Springheart would trust the information when the job was done, and nothing would be able to go wrong.

A pebble dropped beside him. Willowvine was on her way down.

He glanced up from his survey of the grounds to see her perched on the edge of the windowsill, back to him, closing the window. Her hair glinted in the moonlight. She wasn't careful enough about the scarf. If people saw her without it there was no doubt that she was an elf. With the scarf, she could pass as a human child of eight or nine. Her real age of thirty or so, still young for an elf but not a child, was apparent as soon as anyone saw the silvery hair.

As he watched she twisted on her toes and looked down at him. Then she stepped off the ledge, dropping to the second-

P. A. WILSON

floor sill as though it was a step on a deep staircase, hardly landing before she left it to drop beside him.

"In a rush?" he asked as she stood from the crouch.

"There's someone there. Let's go." She tapped her chest as she spoke. The thud let him know she'd been successful.

He grabbed her arm as she moved to run across the lawn. "Let me check it out first."

He still couldn't get her to use caution. If someone was prowling around inside the house, they could easily be in the study, looking out the window, ready to raise the alarm.

When she nodded, he stepped quietly from shadow to shadow until he had a clear view of the window. No outline of a person showed in the glass. He crept back to her and nodded for Willowvine to run for the wall. When she was halfway across, he started his own escape, every second he was in open sight he felt an arrow aimed at his back. They vaulted the wall, coming to rest in its shadow.

He made her stay in place for long enough to catch their breath and to ensure no alarm sounded. Springheart used the time to calm his anger. They never left a job in this kind of hurry unless something was wrong. They never did anything wrong, otherwise they would not be the best in the guild. When they were together, Willowvine followed his guidance. Tonight, she had been on her own. He hadn't liked the idea, but he knew that she was champing to become his equal, and she was in most respects. She was just too much of a risk taker to be truly safe on her own.

The biggest problem he had in keeping her safe was that while she was old enough to be expert at what they did, she was still too young to understand the repercussions of her actions.

Breathing under control, Springheart nudged her. "I'll take the ledger. We don't want it falling out of your shirt in the middle of the street."

Letting go of the grip she had around her chest to hold the

ledger inside her shirt, she wiggled and let the book slide onto her lap. They stored it in the bag, safe until it was delivered to the guildhall.

"There was someone in the house," she said as they stood and began the short walk to the guildhall. "Someone was outside the study."

"So, you decided to just run?" Springheart knew that she wouldn't have run if there was a chance she'd been seen. Hiding was a much better strategy.

She sighed and jabbed him with her elbow. "Yeah, I thought it was best to lead them to you." When he didn't respond, she added, "No. Whoever it was didn't come into the room. And before you ask, I locked the drawer before I left."

Springheart smiled despite his worry. She was good at this, and soon she'd be able to go on solo jobs. It wasn't something he looked forward to. The relationship was a surprise to him. Both of them were orphans, something that got you exiled from elven society, and when they had started working together, after helping to save the world from invasion, he'd expected them to be like brother and sister. It never got there. They were partners almost from the moment they left Madeline's house.

"Did you see that?" Willowvine's voice was low, but alertness sharpened it.

Springheart had seen the shadow that slipped from a doorway to follow them. "Can you sense anything?" Her ability to sense auras had saved their reputations too many times to count.

She took his arm, letting him lead her while her focus was on her magic. It took only a few steps before she was able to answer. "Nothing strong, and it's a bit muddled. There's a feeling of irritation, I guess. Nothing overtly dangerous."

If Willowvine hadn't sensed danger in the spirit of whoever was following, then it could just be someone from the guild. They occasionally sent backup without letting couriers know. Well, it was more like checkup than backup.

P. A. WILSON

"You wanted to talk about something?" If their shadow was from the guild, they could relax, if not, conversation would make them seem like they were not paying attention.

"I'm not sure it's a topic for the street." Willowvine stopped, bent, and fiddled with her bootlaces. She was checking their tail. "He's gone."

"Then you can tell me what you wanted to talk about," Springheart said, knowing that if they didn't get the topic out in the open, she'd start the conversation when he was trying to sleep.

"Are you still okay taking contracts from the guild? Ones we really have no choice but to take?"

This wasn't a new conversation. "If we go freelance, how will we get contracts?"

"I've been thinking about that," she said. "We could talk to previous clients. We could ask them for referrals. Lots of people ask for us. Maybe when we aren't available at the guild, they'll come looking for us."

He tried to look at it with a fresh point of view. He didn't like the fact that the guild told them what to do, but he also knew how hard it was for elves to get work. No matter the reputation they had, people liked to make deals with people who were like them. The guild had representation from all species that might want work done.

All except elves. Elves rarely had a need for the guild's services. When they did, the elves used intermediaries, and even then, they wouldn't want two orphans.

CHAPTER 2

*V*itenkar paced the barracks. He'd managed to gather enough of an army to begin his plans. Taking Cartref for the scree was not going to be an easy campaign. Making the elves extinct would only be the first small victory.

He ordered the soldiers to silence. They obeyed slowly. He would make them regret that. Punish a few and the others would give him more respect, especially if he acted harshly. He might be a merchant, but he still braided the bones of his enemies in his hair. Just because the bones came in a box with the names carved on them, they were no less impressive than if he had ended the life himself.

"You have come to join the glorious battle for this world," he said.

No one cheered.

These were not the best warriors, they were sullen and preferred gaming to training, but he would get them into shape quickly. He would have them eager to do battle soon enough.

He looked out over the group. There were almost fifty scree in the room. They lounged on the beds, or sat in groups huddled around interrupted dice games, or half-drunk bottles of cheap liquor. Few of them had many bones threaded into their braids. New to battle they had yet to gain trophies.

"We have the prize we need to start our campaign," he roared the words as though it was a hard-won victory.

A few of his followers applauded, but most looked like they wanted him to finish so they could return to their games, bottles, or sleep. He couldn't manage them all, the only option was to elevate one or two of them to be his lieutenants, charge them with morale, and punish them if the troops didn't respond as expected.

He looked around for the ones who had applauded. Two of them were watching him with what might be interest. "You, and you," he said, pointing to them. "Meet me in the antechamber. The rest of you go back to your idleness. We will see action soon."

The two scree followed him from the barracks. At the bottom of the great stairs, Vitenkar motioned for them to stop. He strode to the storeroom and checked that the door was locked. The artifact was safely hidden and the door was secure.

"The antechamber," he ordered. The second floor was where he planned his campaign and where he slept. The meeting rooms on the first floor were small and he kept his business papers there. He didn't want his trading activities interrupted. Armies cost money and he couldn't risk losing the men he had, no matter how inferior.

The small antechamber to his bedroom was where he met important clients, and now where he would meet with the few people who would help him to achieve victory. The two scree he'd chosen led the way into the small room. It held a cabinet, where the best of the local wine and liquor were locked, a sofa, and a table large enough to seat six scree, or humans.

"Your names?" he asked as he unlocked the cabinet.

"Dintral, clan Leesot," the shorter one stated immediately.

Vitenkar wondered if he had chosen poorly when the taller one looked him over before answering. "Ballian clan Druth. Why have you asked us here?"

It might be better to work with Ballian, Vitenkar thought. Blind loyalty wasn't always the most useful in a war. Vitenkar offered them wine, and indicated they should sit at the table. He pulled a roll of plans from the back of the cabinet and joined them.

"You know the story about the gate between worlds?" He waited until they nodded. The gate had been unknown to anyone but the elves until five years ago, when a woman had sealed it, saving the world from a violent and catastrophic invasion. "It seems all of Cartref is ready to live a future of peace and harmony."

"Not everyone," Ballian said. "Peace is boring. Look at your soldiers down there. That's the best of what's left of the scree warriors."

Vitenkar smiled. He had chosen well with Ballian. "Exactly. But they are still better warriors than any other race can bring to a battle. The elves have dismantled their armies and turned their energies to teaching and healing."

Dintral snickered. "There's no one left to fight."

Vitenkar glared at Dintral. "That isn't true. The scree are not willing to become traders and farmers. We are warriors."

"So, you want to fight the elves?" Dintral asked.

Vitenkar noticed that Ballian was keeping silent. The man was cunning. He would have to find a use for that. "The elves first."

"Like a tournament?" Dintral asked. "That would be fun. We could have prizes."

"No," Vitenkar shouted, slamming his hand on the table. "This is not a game. The scree will rule this world. The other beings will die or be enslaved."

"That's quite a goal." Ballian sat forward, eager to get started.

"Why the elves first? They are strong in battle and do not flinch from an army."

Vitenkar took a long sip of his wine. He did not want to be interrupted again. In the pause, he stared down both of his lieutenants, cowing them into listening. When he felt they were sufficiently attentive he started explaining. "The elves don't reproduce often. I have found a way to stop them from having any children at all. We need only cut down the existing villages. They will be easy to eradicate. They will stand as an example of our might. Other species will surrender to avoid our wrath. And if we battle them first, we will not face them in every fight as they foolishly come to the aid of the others."

"Who will be next?" Dintral asked.

"When will we know the elves are gone?" asked Ballian. "They may have laid down arms, but they fight to the death when they engage. If we have to kill all of the living elves, we'll need a bigger army."

Vitenkar had thought long and hard about this. Ballian was correct. The elves would not die easily. But they only needed to kill enough to dishearten the rest. "They will only fight as long as they have hope. As soon as they realize there are no more children, they will stop fighting. We will attack the first three villages as soon as the men are in battle condition. By then the elders, at least, will have noticed that there are no more conceptions."

"How have you stopped them?" Ballian asked.

It had been so easy that Vitenkar was tempted to embellish the story. But he decided to save it for the troops. These two men were his trusted lieutenants. They would get the truth. "They are tied to this land. There is a place where their fate is written on a stone. I have removed this stone." He didn't tell them that he'd tortured and killed ten seers to get the information he needed to find this place. Or that he hadn't gone himself, but had hired, and then slain, a mercenary.

* * *

WILLOWVINE AND SPRINGHEART receive a mysterious contract to locate a vital artifact. Use the QR code to grab your copy of The Eleven Stones: family and save the elves.

FREE EBOOK

Claim your copy of Obstacles of Magic when you use the QR code to sign up for my newsletter and learn more about Madeline's history with magic.

ALSO BY P A WILSON

For more books by P A Wilson

Use the QR code below or go to pawilson.ca

ABOUT THE AUTHOR

Perry Wilson is a Canadian author based in Vancouver, BC who has big ideas and an itch to tell stories. Having spent some time on university, a career, and life in general, she returned to writing in 2008 and hasn't looked back since (well, maybe a little, but only while parallel parking).

She is a member of the Vancouver Writers Social Group, The Royal City Literary Arts Society, and The Surrey Writing Workshop. Perry has self-published several novels. She writes the Madeline Journeys, a fantasy series about a high-powered lawyer who finds herself trapped in a magical world, the Quinn Larson Quests, which follows the adventures of a wizard named Quinn who must contend with volatile fae in the heart of Vancouver, and the Charity Deacon Investigations, a mystery thriller series about a private eye who tends to fall into serious trouble with her cases, and The Riverton Romances, a series based in a small town in Oregon, one of her favorite states. Her stand-alone novels are Breaking the Bonds, Closing the Circle, and The Dragon at The Edge of The Map.

For more information
www.pawilson.ca
pawilson@pawilson.ca

ACKNOWLEDGMENTS

People think that the process of writing is solitary. That's not the case for me. I have help from so many people it would be hard to acknowledge everyone, but I'll give it a try.

The support and inspiration I get from my writer's groups is incalculable. The Vancouver Writers Social Group opens my mind to other ways of telling a story. The Royal City Literary Arts Society gives me the opportunity to meet and share with other writers who have more knowledge than I do. The Other 11 Months group is where I learn about getting the words on the page. And my critique group who helps me find the best parts of the story I want to tell. Thanks to all of the members of these great groups.

Last of all, but definitely a huge part of the process, my beta readers. These are the people who love stories and are willing, and more than able, to tell me if my finished story is ready for you, my readers.